NEVER TOO LATE

Jo Barney

Penner
PUBLISHING

Los Angeles, California

This edition published by
Penner Publishing
Post Office Box 57914
Los Angeles, California 91413

www.pennerpublishing.com

ISBN 13: 978-1-940811-36-9
eISBN 13: 978-1-940811-35-2

Cover Designer: Christa Holland, Paper & Sage Designs

Years ago, Annie Proulx, author of The Shipping News, *said that she absorbed the language and speech of Newfoundland by sitting in coffee shops and listening. She added, as I recall, "I could sit and listen for hours. No one ever notices an old lady in the next booth." Another author, Elizabeth Berg, advises, in* The Day I Ate Whatever I Wanted and Other Small Acts of Liberation *"wear a hat and some old lady shoes, and you can do whatever you want."*

My book, Never Too Late, *is dedicated to all those feisty old ladies who know about the liberation that comes with being unnoticed, and the exhilaration that results from doing whatever they want. I know and admire a couple of women like that and this book is an attempt to get to that place also.*

It is never too late to be what you might have been.

—GEORGE ELIOT

PROLOGUE

"Yeah?" a voice asks when he rings the bell.

"I've got something nice for you," he answers.

A buzzer lets him in, and he finds Patsy's door open at the top of the stairs.

Inside, a tattered blind defends the only window. A woman, gray irises glowing beneath heavy eyelids, greets him from a narrow bed pushed against one wall. "One hundred dollars," she says as she lifts a bottle to her lips. She frowns, shakes it, and sets it down on the table beside her.

Art knows the minute he sees her sprawled across the bed, her privates showing, her robe ties clutching loosely at her waist, her voice soggy with drugs or alcohol or both, that he has made a mistake. There'll be no talking to her.

She wheezes. "You said you got something nice for me. Where is it?"

"In my pocket. Fifty dollars, your going rate, Patsy." He pulls a wad of bills out of his back pocket. "I heard you were worth it."

"Yeah? From who?"

"Someone who said you're really hot." Nice touch, he congratulates himself. Maybe there's still a chance to negotiate with her. Not about the sex. He can't imagine doing it, but about the blackmail. "Can I sit down for a minute?"

"Sure, it's Christmas isn't it? I've been doing a little celebrating." She shoves her body upright on her pillow, reaches with a dark, unsteady hand toward a second bottle on the nightstand. "Drink?"

Art has already had a couple of drinks, to get his courage up, before he drove to the street his son Brian had described. He's glad he did. Patsy, her pale eyes now dimming under lowering eyelids, her boobs deflated at the edge of each armpit, her fingers touching herself as if they have a mind of their own, makes him shudder. He glances away from her, takes in the emptiness of the room.

A narrow bed presses against one wall. He slides a pile of clothes off a wooden chair and moves it closer to her. As he sits down, he knocks against a small sink stacked with bowls, a hot plate next to it. This hole is her home, not just a place of business. She pours a plastic tumbler half full of bourbon and leans forward to offer it to him, and he accepts it with a shrug.

"Like I said, it's Christmas. And you look a little nervous." When his fingers misfire and he spills some of the liquor on his pants, she caws a laugh and lifts the bottle again. "Come on, we don't have all night...or do we? Hundred dollars, all night."

"Let me finish my drink," he says, and he drains his glass and looks for a place to put it. It slips and bounces on the floor. He doesn't need any more alcohol; he's slurring almost as much she is. And if he doesn't do this fast, he'll not even remember why he is here. "I'm not sure I can get it up. I'm a little drunk, and I'm really tired. I haven't slept good the past couple of days." He sits back, trying to gather the words he needs.

Patsy pokes under her pillow, pulls out a plastic tube, rattles it. "I use these when I need some sleep." She pries off the lid, palms a few capsules, and holds her hand out to him, pulls it back. "After the fifty bucks, of course." She shrugs. "Oh, hell, it's Christmas." She leans over the edge of the bed, tucks the pills into his jacket pocket, and flops back against the pillow. "Damn, I don't feel so hot."

She sprawls like a rag doll across the mattress, the whites of her eyes flashing as she blinks and lowers her lids, moans.

Art glances at her drink, lifts it to his lips, and wonders what he should do next. Cover her up at least. He stands up, pulls her robe over her crotch and breasts, and yanks at the blanket under her feet, but he can't budge it. Patsy snores with a soft purr. She'll be out for a long time, he decides. He has to get home. Edith will kill him if he misses the family's Christmas brunch. He stumbles toward the door, and his arm brushes against a little Christmas tree sitting on the counter. Plastic. Earrings and satin-and-paper ribbons droop from its skinny branches. Even Patsy needs a tree, he thinks. A plastic ribbon catches between his fingers, and he's not sure why, but he slides it into his pants pocket. Then he hears the woman stir, throw up, the vomit splashing on the floor. He smells the stink, and he doesn't look back. Escaping through the doorway, what is left of her drink still in his hand, he feels his way down the dark stairs. He is hammered, but he has to talk to Brian, let him know that his father has failed him.

CHRISTMAS MORNING, 1993

I wake up with a pop, the kind of jolt that informs me that I'm through sleeping, even if I close my eyes and try to bring back the warm arms that had wrapped around me, the music swirling behind my eyes. What I usually hear when I wake from this sort of dream is a raspy wind rushing through Art's narrow nostrils, the angry snort that accompanies it, rattling the innerspring mattress that holds us afloat. This morning Art lies on his side, the snores silent.

Lately, whenever I wake up too early and try to sink back into a little more sleep, memories pick at me. Right now it is the memory of lying on a different mattress, one crunching with straw. I have not thought of that old mattress in years. What other almost-forgotten scene will emerge, depress me, if I don't stretch my legs? I have to move and trust that the usual cramp will relent, that I'll be able to roll out from under the quilt and step into my slippers without going down on one knotted knee.

My feet brush the lump of soap that is under the bottom sheet. My thighs pull my knees up to my stomach, but I'm not quite ready to straighten my legs, get out of bed.

The night Art found the bar of Ivory soap in our bed, he sneered at me, more of a twitch of his thin upper lip, as if he could barely hold back a ha. For leg cramps, I tried to explain. It was in the Oregonian. As usual, that scornful ha. Like the time he smelled the alcohol on my breath from the nine gin-soaked golden raisins that I had pulled out of the jar with a toothpick. For arthritis, the article said. Ha, Art said. And like last week when I suggested having the young new neighbors over for Christmas punch, and he blew out a loud puff of air before I could finish my sentence.

I close my eyes, remembering about the worst ha of all, that one last Fall. I'd read an article about people going back to college, not college really but the free classes offered for anyone over sixty-five at the university downtown. Maybe anthropology? I thought out loud. His lip curled. "Don't be so stupid."

I pull the comforter over my shoulder and try to stop this digging into the past, a habit I can overcome by forcing myself to get up. But I need a little more sleep before I face this day. Christmas morning. And my daughter-in-law, Kathleen. As usual, her fingers will wrench the potato peeler from mine, will take the old knife out of my hands as I slice the onions, will grab the garlic in the garlic thing and squeeze just once more. She'll remind me, ever so gently, that the strata smells a little burnt. Kathleen believes she is being helpful. My son Brian, oblivious, now twisting in some sort of midlife whirl of his own, will pass his lips over my cheek as he opens my front door, will not hear me say as we touch, "I love you," his eyes focused on the destructive small brood he has produced as it races to the packages under the tree.

Relief overwhelmed me a year ago on Christmas Day as I called out a final goodbye to my son's family, their shopping bags full of shirts and electronic games, three hours after the morning had erupted. I leaned back against the closed door, breathed, and saw Art slumped in his lounger asleep, avoiding the chaos, as usual.

I poke a foot out from under a tangled sheet. Find some joy! yesterday's horoscope had advised me. Right now, I'll settle for coffee. The air is morning-warm, the furnace groaning somewhere under me. I push the covers to one side, turn toward Art's flannelled back, the wall he builds between us when he comes to our bed.

I know I'm being mean-spirited, a disposition Christmas always delivers like a seasonal virus. Joy, I tell myself again and touch Art's hump of a shoulder, give it a poke. If I have to get up, layer the cheese strata, set the table, pick up yesterday's newspapers, he at least can help by turning on the tree lights and starting the fire in the fireplace. Shit! I've forgotten the stockings. They, and the stuff I've collected to fill them over the past six months, are piled in a box in the closet. I shake him a little harder. "Get up!"

Art rolls over on his back. His blue eyes stare up at the ceiling fixture hanging above his head. His mouth is open, as if he's about to snore, but he isn't rasping, gurgling, even blinking.

I raise myself up on an elbow. I pat his arm, bring my hand up to touch his cheek. His skin feels like that of an unripe peach, hard under whiskery fuzz. Cold.

"Art?"

My ear grazes his mouth as I listen for a breath. Silence. I press my hand against his chest, feel his pajama buttons with shaking fingers.

"Art?"

Art is dead.

It isn't as if I never imagined him dying, leaving me to finish my life alone. At those times, the idea hadn't been frightening, maybe even the opposite. A new life for me once he was gone, I envisioned, a better life, maybe. But this actual moment is not part of that scene. I drop my head back to my pillow and try to figure out what to do.

My breath isn't taking hold. I seem to be leaking at the seams, lungs empty, about to be as dead as Art. I force my mouth to open, suck in air, push it out in a whoosh. The morning scrambles into focus: the unfilled socks, the strata, the fire, the tree lights. The dead man lying beside me. Three miles away, the grandchildren have gotten up, already wild with anticipation, are racing around, knocking each other about, not hearing their mother's threats from the bathroom, not noticing their father's clenched jaw, determined to get through the morning.

Like me, my son does not like Christmas. Genetic, we almost-joked last year, over a too-sweet eggnog as we watched Meg and Winston squabble about a useless toy, pieces of it already lost in the piles of colored tissue. Standing over us, Kathleen, her lips gripped in her steady, motherly smile, sent an unmistakable time-to-go look to her husband and gathered up the strewn toys.

I close my eyes. Christmas is difficult, but Christmas with a dead person as its centerpiece will be unbearable. Brian, a kind, open man, a good son, too sensitive, really, will have to deal with the unopened gifts piled in front of a cold fireplace, his disappointed children's howls, his stalwartly competent wife patting his arm as he tries to find a way to say goodbye to a father who has remained a stranger to the end.

I know I can get through what's next—I'm not crying, maybe won't ever—but I'm sure Brian hasn't rehearsed this death as I have. I feel a flush of a plan, and I sit up, search for my glasses. Yes. I will put Art aside for a day. I will tuck the comforter up around his chin, explain that he's sick, shut the bedroom door, and go ahead with the morning's ordeal. "Don't wake Grandpa," I'll warn the children. I'll let the wife meddle in the brunch, try not to care when the boy and girl tear open their gifts like little savages, hide their uneaten casserole under their napkins, whine as they edge toward the door, bounty in hand. I'll wave at them as they climb into their car, leaving red-and-green garbage for me to clean up. I will whisper, as always, "I love you," to my son as he raises a goodbye hand from the open car window. Then, after they disappear, I will call someone to take care of Art.

Yes, it can go that way.

I glance at my husband. He is still staring. I should close his eyes. With my thumb, I push down the lids, am relieved that they stay down. I get out of bed, find my glasses on the floor, turn back to the man I've left behind—no, who's left me behind—and arrange the comforter over him.

On my way to the bathroom, I kick against his abandoned shoes, and I bend to pick up them up, along with his dirty socks, and at that moment I understand that the plan won't work. Nothing has changed. Art, and all of his carelessness, is still here. His ghost will wander the house, lips twitching. He will continue to make his ha sound at me. Later, after the strata, I will say goodbye at the door. Behind me, he will have sunk into his chair and fallen asleep.

I'll be angry as usual but at a ghost who won't give a damn about us any more dead than he did alive.

I set the shoes in Art's closet, go to the kitchen, to the telephone.

The ambulance arrives just as I am pulling my sweatshirt over my head. I fluff the sleep mats out of my hair and open the door. The men, their stiff blue uniforms shielding them from whatever they might find in my house, follow my pointing finger, and moments later, Art is on the gurney. They cover his face with a sheet, fill out a form, and tell me where I can find him when I am ready to make arrangements.

"Are you all right?" they ask. "Do you have someone to call?"

They look at me, seem to expect something more, tears, maybe. "I'm fine," I answer. "I have a son."

The older man touches my shoulder, his mouth curving in a practiced way. "Call him." He squeezes my arm and follows the others out the door.

I go to the bedroom, see that some time in all this, Art has wet the bed. I pull off the sheets and cases, carry them to the washing machine, stuff them in.

Art is dead. I need to fill the stockings, hang them up.

Art is dead. I take the Christmas box out of the closet and set it on the hearth. A plastic doll with boobs stretches a manicured hand out to me.

Art is dead. A chocolate Santa goes in the grandboy's sock. I imagine the hubbub when he peels off the foil and bites off its head before he's eaten breakfast.

Art is dead. Four adult stockings lump in the bottom of the box, and I drop face cream and razorblades and Starbucks gift cards into their hollows.

Art is dead. I hang up all six stockings, even Art's, on the hooks that have hidden under the mantel since that first child-filled Christmas morning in this house years ago.

Art is dead. Hands heavy against my knees, I push myself up from my squat in front of the fireplace and notice the bag of candy canes. "It's Christmas," I'll say, when Kathleen frowns. I tuck one into each furry white cuff.

I am finished. I phone Brian.

"Art is dead." The words fling themselves against the phone's mouthpiece, fly back to my cheeks like sharp stones, bring a bitter glaze to my eyes. I blink, say, "Yes, he's been taken away." It seems important to add, "We can still do the stockings for the children."

Brian arrives alone twenty minutes later, doesn't wait for me to answer the door bell, rushes in. "I love you," I whisper as he takes me in his arms, holds me tighter than I've been held in a long time, maybe forever.

2

At first I hand over the reins to Kathleen who would have taken them from me anyway, and she holds a firm grip on the days that follow. She manages the social decisions, the memorial, the reservation for a reception room. In his usual quiet, competent way, Brian manages the details at the mortuary, details I'm not willing to deal with, except to show him Art's and my written directions to be cremated and buried on the one burial site we bought years ago, big enough for both of us if we were in small containers, calling lists of friends, talking to Herbert Smith, Art's attorney about the legal aspects of death. Every once in a while, my son walks by as I lie in Art's lounger with my feet up and my eyes closed. I feel him touch my shoulder, and I shake my head. I am thinking. Not about Christmas morning. Art's gray, staring face doesn't need to be thought about. On its own, it slides across my eyes, lids open or shut, like a floater.

No, I am remembering other Arts, bubbling up from a dank well somewhere near my belly, ancient moments as painful in the replay as they were in reality, and I'm back on the shadowy path that leads me to a young girl with bobbed dark hair and the third-highest grades in her graduating class. She didn't get to give a speech like the other two, but she received a scholarship to Minnetanka Normal School. That girl believed she'd be a teacher.

Then she got pregnant.

"It's your own fault," my mother hissed, the furrow in her forehead narrowing her eyes into angry slits. My lack of monthly cotton rags on the clothesline had forced the truth out of me. "You should have said no." She grabbed my wrist and yanked.

But who could have resisted the beer-fueled pleas of the best-looking tenor in the church choir? Almost the only one, unlike his friends, saved from going into the service by his flat feet. Two years older. Employed. Any day now going to buy the gas station where he worked the three-to-ten shift. "War's over. Everyone will be getting cars, needing gas," he assured me as we squirmed in the backseat of his father's

Plymouth sedan and found each other's parts, the midnight sky eventually lightening with dawn.

The night I told him we had to get married, Art, looking for something important just over my head, ran a hand across his oiled pompadour and said, "I guess that's it." On our wedding day, my mother-in-law stepped close to me, offering not a hug but a nudge, and murmured into my ear, "He will be a difficult man to live with. He's just like his father."

Soon Art's father died, and his mother went off to a daughter's house to be cared for. The daughter got the furniture. We got the old mattress. Art said we should, so we carried it to our little rental house, stuffed it with the hay left over from the cow that had also moved on and gave the ugly bag a try. But after a few days, and cringing at what those circles and blobs of stains would reveal if they could talk, I spent an hour spreading the straw over the winter garden out in back. That evening we bought a new mattress, and our living room was heated by flames licking at ancient striped ticking. Art didn't like to waste anything.

Other shards of broken dreams poke at me as I give myself over to the fragments of my life. The first time he grunted, "Go to hell," through clenched teeth at me, slammed the door, didn't come back until morning. The screeching of a shoved-back chair and a shout, "Fuck! Didn't I tell you to stop crying?" to an unhappy two-year-old. The Formica kitchen table overturning, our hamburgers skidding across the linoleum, as he swung a fist at a sneering, teen-aged Brian. The night, nights, he rocked the bed as he worked his penis after I'd said no.

Art had become a disappointed, angry man.

I search, empty-handed, for the times I loved him. I doubt he ever loved me. He accepted, as his due for taking me and a child on, the folded clean clothes waiting in the chest of drawers; the meat-and-potato dinners on the table each night at six; the waxed floors and, later, the vacuumed wall-to-wall carpet. I accepted, in those early years, his walking out of our lives every morning; his stoic returns; his weekly dispersals in the tan budget envelope marked House-hold, the same envelope for years, the folds growing thin and fuzzy and finally splitting open; his plans for our occasional vacations in whatever Plymouth he was driving. And, at first, I accepted my loneliness, and then later, my own anger that festered under the surface of my days.

His gaze did not wander from the TV screen the night I gathered the words, asked him if he loved me. "Every day I go to work, come home, pay for our food and house. Isn't that enough?"

No, it hadn't been enough. I push against the back of Art's lounger, and my feet rise up a few more inches. Not then, not now.

Sometimes, though, it had seemed almost enough. The few summers when we had saved money and could take a couple of weeks off and escape our life, if not each other.

Times we looked over the edge of a crater, a crack in the earth, at an orange sun sinking into blue water, mesmerized by beauty so foreign to our own narrow vista at home. I can still feel the moment at Estes Park when his arm wrapped my shoulders, his warm hand brushing my breast. "Beautiful," I whispered. Then the word, the look, the touch, like rising mists, dissipated in the cold air between us. He reached for his camera and pointed to the spot I should stand. The photo was later pasted onto a black page in a fake-leather–bound album, date noted, and the book was shut and stored on a closet shelf.

I pulled out a couple of those old photo albums this week, massaging the painful memories they contain with the soothing pictures of a grinning boy wearing a broad band of Scout badges, later grinning again under a square black cap, diploma held in front of his chest, Brian working hard to please me, to ease the bitter marriage he had been born into. But I ran out of good times and the bad times slinked in as I turned the pages, moments that hadn't been caught on Kodak film, moments filed in an overflowing folder marked Guilt, a folder tucked between a couple of my brain cells that still flicker at irregular intervals. Like the moment Art called me a slut.

I don't want to think anymore.

Someone is running the vacuum in the hall. The grandgirl, I suppose. Meg. Of the two children, she pleases me to the most, probably because she reminds me of myself, a busy, tidy girl whose attempt to please others is already carving permanent creases in her forehead.

"Sorry. Did I wake you up, Grandma?"

Kathleen, her hands wet from whatever she's been doing in the kitchen, wheels the vacuum away. "Meg, I told you to not vacuum where Grandma is resting." Meg's frown deepens.

"I was dreaming, Meg. Not good dreams. I'm glad you woke me up."

"I have bad dreams." Meg leans on the arm of my chair. "Dreams I have to wake myself up from. Mom says it's because I ate something I shouldn't have."

"Maybe. Or maybe it's because you've done something you shouldn't have." I suspect this isn't an idea anyone, especially a grandmother, should suggest to a child.

But Meg understands. "Or maybe both? Like yesterday when I found where Winston had hidden the rest of his chocolate Santa and I ate it?"

"Yes, sometimes it's both." I crank the chair upright and reach for the Good Housekeeping on the end table. Meg stands by my side, waiting perhaps to be invited to squeeze in, to share the pages with me as she used to when she was little. She pretends she doesn't notice that my eyes are focused on an Olay ad, and after a moment, she turns, calls, "Where's Winston, Mom? He still has to do his chores."

I listen as the girl's footsteps recede; the back door bangs. I don't know why I can't do them, the grandmotherly things that should come without thought. I have lost my ability to feel unconditional love. I probably never did have it, just acted the roles handed to me over the years. I flip through the magazine until I reach the essay at the last page. I've always enjoyed these short snapshots of other women's lives. Today's piece describes the pain of losing a faithful dog to old age, the author's tears most likely staining the page as she wrote.

I am envious of those tears, the fact that someone can put a loss like that into words, salving the wound, finding solace. I can't do that, can't even imagine myself picking up a pen. How does one describe an empty vessel?

3

I find a handkerchief, the one my mother gave me on my wedding day, its old lace yellowed, in the top drawer of my dresser. I won't need it probably, but perhaps someone else will. I tuck it in my purse. I glance at the mirror over the sink, and I see an old lady patting down her wild, gray hair. I will put on a little lipstick. The black pantsuit makes my skin sallow, but I won't add any other color, no jewelry; a widow is expected to be bereaved, at least until her husband is safely in the ground, the mourners fed, the house cleared.

Ten minutes later, Brian, standing at the black limousine's open door, waits for me to slide in. "Did we have to do this?" I am not sure to whom he's talking.

"Yes," Kathleen answers from a far corner in the back seat. The children are patting the leather, working at opening a cabinet door. "It's expected, even when the service is at the gravesite. So the family does not have to be concerned with driving, parking, all that."

Art has been dead almost two weeks, and something has held up his burial. I'm not sure what, but I am glad that it is happening now rather than during those first days I hadn't been able to raise myself from the lounger. I slide in next to my daughter-in-law, who is tucking a Kleenex into her sleeve.

"In case you need it," she says, and I realize the tissue is intended for me. "I hope all this is okay with you. We all talked about a family-only graveside ceremony because Art wasn't the religious type, and you seemed all right with the idea. I've arranged for the reception in the mortuary's Garden Room for friends. The caterer is very good, but I'm not sure whether I should have ordered the wine—"

"We need wine," I interrupt. "I'm assuming a few bottles, at least." For me, I want to add, but I know that most of the attendees will also be drinkers, just as Art was. Red. I prefer white. "You did order white, of course?" I say, and then I shut up. This isn't my show. I just need a little white wine to get through it.

"Of course, Edith. And the shrimp Art loved."

Art didn't love shrimp, did he? I lean back against the seat and try to remember. No. Art loved meat and potatoes.

I love shrimp. I consider how, in Kathleen's mind, Art and Edith have apparently melded together, both shrimp lovers, both also dead or close to it.

"That's nice," I say.

"Hey, Mom," Winston calls. "This limo is brand new! 1996, this says." He waves a brochure in front of his mother's eyes and she tells him to put whatever he has found back or the driver will be angry. The boy watches the steady black cap in front of him as he folds the paper. His sister rubs her index fingers at him. Shame, she signals and giggles. They open another cabinet, find the little bottles of liquor possibly left over from the last voyagers in this landship. A wedding, perhaps, or a high school prom. They hold them up, demanding a taste. Kathleen gives her husband her do-something frown, Brian in return answering, "What?" in his recent Brian-is-out-of-it way.

Kathleen takes the bottles from the children, replaces them in the cabinet, and says, "No," in a voice I know they'll remember. I have often admired that trait in other women, the ability to say no so that others hear and know that they mean it.

We arrive at a green hill pockmarked with flat markers. I remember the Memorial Day visits to my grandmother's grave, when my duty as the youngest child was to clip the grass at the edges of her gravestone before I poked the metal container holding the peonies into the grass beneath her name. The cemetery would be filled with children and parents who, once they said another hello or goodbye to their dead relatives, chatted and ran among the red and pink and green spots of color.

We five are almost alone on this burial ground. No peonies, no sprouts of grass to be taken care of. A cold mist fills the air. The small white tent on a rise at the side of a winding path must be our destination, and Brian takes my arm and leads me toward it. A woman in a flowing dress, a stranger, meets us on the path and asks, "Aren't we glad it's stopped raining?" Not waiting for an answer, she continues, "The children have a poem? No? A song?" They grin yes, and the woman hurries ahead of us.

Meg and Winston have decided on "You Are My Sunshine," the only song anyone has ever heard Art sing, perhaps the only one he learned from his mother as she soothed a difficult child. He used to mouth the words, whisper them, actually, walking to the grocery store or working in the garden. The song probably accompanied him those nights he escaped our house. "Got to get some air!" he'd say, as the front door closed.

Until that last morning. Don't, I tell myself, and the children's willowy humming saves me from going over that ground yet another time as we approach the gravesite. At the entrance of the tent, the woman waits, and when Brian comes closer, she steps out and pulls him aside. I can't hear what she is saying, but the look on Brian's face tells me something is not right.

The two of them turn, and with a sweep of her hand, she welcomes us into the tent and suggests that a few words from Brian might precede the children's song. He looks at me and then at Kathleen, who is shaking her head at the skirmishing at her side. "Let's do it," he says, a flash of his father's grim determination darkening his face. He steps to the edge of a straight-edged rectangle cut into the grass, and as we reach for each other's hands, he begins to speak. His gentle goodbye fills the air with a vision of a father, husband, grandfather seen through a haze of regret, anger, and love of the sort that lurks unfelt until moments like this one. Brian proves himself up to this difficult task, his eyes filling with his last sentence. A perfect son at a not-so-perfect father's funeral.

The attendants use ribbons to lower a small granite urn into its burial place. I locate the shovel that Kathleen has instructed me to use, step to the waiting pile of soil, and I pour a small scoop into the grass-edged opening. It is only when two childish voices rise above the crunch of small rocks striking the stone lid that I feel my eyes dim. I hand the shovel to one of the helpers and take out the hankie I thought I wouldn't need. "You make me happy when skies are gray..." The irony of the song's words brings me to my knees, where the black gabardine of my pants captures the muddy moment.

Kathleen moans, "Oh God," places an arm under my elbow and lifts me upright. I want to shake her off, but I don't have the strength.

People have gathered in the Garden Room. Brian greets them, thanks them for helping the family move through this sad day, and he comments about his father's serious work ethic, his long marriage, and his lifelong avoidance of large gatherings. He raises his glass to the twenty or so faces watching him, a few hoping perhaps for the necessary little funereal joke, and says, "He'd like this gathering just fine. I can hear him say, 'That's just what I wanted, a few friends waving goodbye, a glass of wine in the other hand. '" His small audience does chuckle, responds the toast, turns to voices nearby, perhaps not as impressed as I am with my son's Art voice.

I don't know most of these people: some are from the post office whom I met perhaps once at some employees' gathering, a cluster of my son's friends, unknown to me but solicitous in that half-smile, funeral way as eyes meet, ask, behind my back, How long do we have to stay? I hear myself assuring the concerned faces looming too close to mine that I am all right, that yes, he was a good man, that my husband is at peace as I bring the glass of white wine to my lips. After the second glass, I even manage to offer my cheek for a consoling kiss from several of the guests. Lynne hugs me, nearly tipping me off my feet, as she whispers, "I'll call soon." I had thought that one or two of my other friends would come, but perhaps they don't read the obituaries as carefully as I do. I probably should have called them. Who knows what the rules for this occasion are?

Then the reception is over, and we are back in the limo. Silent and only kicking each other a little until their mother waves her hand at them, the children lie back against the soft cushions. I look out at the passing cars. Brian's eyes are closed, still probably coming to terms with his several good-byes.

Kathleen leans across Meg's lap and asks, "Who was that that man in the tweed jacket standing on the terrace? I didn't get to meet him. A friend?"

I shake my head. "I didn't notice him. Maybe someone from the mortuary. Do you know, Brian?"

His eyes still closed, he shrugs. "I'm not sure."

4

A woman-sized lounger, in light blue, arrives the next morning, and the deliveryman takes the old one away. He has
decided it is too worn for resale. "Maybe Goodwill," he suggests.

"Whatever," I tell him. "I'm glad to have a chair that
fits me, finally." I've done some rearranging in the past several days. Bags of Art's clothes line the hallway on their way
to a homeless shelter. This morning I cleared the bathroom
cabinet of the many plastic bottles and tubes and lozenges
that Art had accumulated over the years, and the containers
fill the wastebasket at the bathroom door. I read somewhere
that one should not flush medicines down the toilet, but I

can't remember how the Oregonian recommended to dispose of them. Bury them in coffee grounds? Someplace you could take them? Do homeless men need them? I don't have to decide right now. Instead, Brian will be picking me up soon to go see a financial advisor, and I need to collect a few of the papers that Art piled in his desk drawers.

The doorbell rings, and I have my coat and the folder in my hands, but when I open the door, I see that Brian has someone with him. "You came here? I thought we'd be going to your office," I say to the man I assume is the advisor. Why does he look familiar?

"Mom, this is Sergeant Durrell. He wants to talk with you. About Dad."

I open the door wider. "I don't understand."

"I insisted that I be here when he came to talk to you. It's pretty ridiculous." Brian lets the policeman step through the doorway. "Let's just get it over with." I lead them to the living room sofa. I sit down in my lounger. If I'm reading Brian's tone right, I shouldn't offer this man a cup of coffee.

Brian takes charge, disgust and anger tingeing his words. "Dad died unexpectedly without any known physical reason. This being the case, when they took him to the hospital's morgue, the law required an autopsy be performed to determine the cause of death. The coroner's office called to tell you that this would occur before they released him for cremation, and I answered the phone and said I'd let you know." Brian pauses, looks at me, and I give him a you're-in-charge shrug. "This process held up the service a few days. I didn't tell you because I didn't want to stress you any more than you already were. Besides, I was certain they'd discover a heart problem, like we'd guessed, and that would be it."

He runs his hand through his hair, his father's gesture, a similarity that I hadn't noticed in the past. "It nearly was. Dad's heart showed indications of a massive heart attack, as the death certificate stated. But they also took some tissue and blood samples. The results came back the day of the funeral." He glances at the police officer, who is opening a pad he's been holding.

Tissue? Blood? Why? I'm suddenly listening.

"We did a couple of tests." The officer is reading his notes. "Your husband's remains showed traces of Valium, along with some barbiturates, Mrs. Finlay. Combined with the 1.5 alcohol level the lab found in his blood, a drug over-dose might be involved in his death." He takes a pen from his shirt pocket, clicks it. "What do you know about his drug usage?"

"That's ridiculous." Drugs? Art had a few prescriptions, an over-enthusiasm for supplements, in my opinion, aspirin, vitamin E, like everyone else. Drugs? "His doctor had him on Lipitor and something else." I nearly stumble as I push myself upright and step around the lounger's footstool. "The bottles and tubes are in the wastebasket, if you want to see them." I can't make sense of what I've just heard. Art. Valium? Barbiturates? Only movie stars die of stuff like that.

I bring in the basket of vials and drop it in front of the sergeant. "I was about to throw these out." I feel my face heating up. "My husband's dead. His heart gave out. No matter what else you have found, he's still dead of a bad heart, isn't he?"

"I'm sure we'll figure it out, Mrs. Finlay." A heavy man, he sighs a little as he strains to stand. "An insurance company has let us know they are interested in our findings." He tucks his pad back into his jacket pocket and picks up the rattling basket. He looks back at us without offering his hand. "Thanks. We'll talk again."

Once the door closes, I turn to Brian, so angry my lips are paralyzed. "He was at the service, wasn't he, that man?" I force the words out. "He wanted to stop us from putting Art in the ground—for more tests? On a dead man's ashes? Or, my God, had that policeman just delivered the ashes after they were tested in a police lab?" The idea is so sickening I feel as if I'm vomiting words. "Why didn't you tell me? Do you believe I couldn't handle the idea that your father may have killed himself, that the death certificate might be changed to read suicide?"

"Mom—"

"No, don't. Art was a contrary, selfish man. Suicide would be a terrific punishment for a family and a life he hated. We'd be forever guilty of a wrongdoing only he understood." Of their own accord, my fists thrash out toward my son's chest; his hands open, catch mine. "I could kill him for that!" Then I hear what I've just said and my voice crumbles into a gag of a gasp. A ha of my own, I think, tightening my shoulders, pulling my hands back to myself. "Oh, Brian. I wonder what hell your father will take us to next."

5

Art's clothes, dumped out of the bags, fill the hallway. I perch on a footstool, my knees almost to my shoulders, and I reach into the pile in front of me. My fingers sneak into pockets, feeling for whatever is lurking in their corners. I'm searching for answers to a mystery trailing in the wake of a dead man's body, still making waves weeks later. The policeman has not called, Brian only shakes his head at my questions, at my quest for the truth, and I know I'll not rest until I know what Art was up to.

When I find something, not a stick of gum but something that might lead me in some direction—a matchbook cover, suspicious because Art didn't smoke, a business card, a wad of pink Kleenex, a dollar bill with a telephone number scribbled on it—I place the clue in a large manila envelope retrieved from Art's desk. Not the budget envelope, which was the first thing I tossed when I cleaned his den, but a new one on which I have written WHY? with a Sharpie pen.

By the time I've gone through all the pockets, have emptied the drawers in his desk, and have flipped through the pages of the books on his bookcase, I know what I have to do next.

Brian thinks I'm nuts. Not that he says anything. Kathleen, however, because they have talked, informs me that she believes my search for answers is therapeutic, only a little nuts. If I need help, call, and she assures me she'll come by and help sort it all out. But my daughter-in-law, who is convinced she knows more than everyone else, didn't know Art. I, his own wife, apparently didn't know him either. The not-knowing fuels the obsession which has taken me over. I have to find out who and what killed him.

Because, my hands in his pockets, my fingers digging into his corners, I'm beginning to suspect the culprit might be me. My unlove of him. I didn't hand him the barbiturates, of course, but my coldness might have driven him to them. Or to the Valium. Depressed for most of the years I lived with him, my husband never admitted to his dark side nor did he do anything to change his dour view of life. Despite his disposition, he maintained a steady course, working, coming home, managing our lives in his cold, efficient way for forty years. Why, then, a few months ago, had he begun leaving at night, coming home a few hours later with alcohol on his breath, going silent when I asked where he'd been and why? Could I be the cause of this change in Art, of his death? Maybe. I couldn't remember the one moment that might have pushed him over the edge, but the accumulation of bitter years, and the thousands of angry, silent moments, might have been miserable enough to convince him that life wasn't worth living.

I can relate to that thought.

I spread the pocket scraps over the top of Art's desk and begin to sort through them. I put a couple of matchbook covers from bars or restaurants, a card with an unfamiliar name and business printed on it, the dollar bill, smoothed out, in plastic bag. I paperclip some Visa receipts and a few handwritten notes, numbers on them lined up behind dollar signs. The notes especially puzzle me, as does the pink Kleenex, each of which I stuff into another bag. Since I was taking the time to empty his pockets anyway, I save the coins I find and toss them into the glass that once held Art's before-dinner bourbon. Then I wonder what next? Instead of eliminating a mystery, I seem to be feeding one.

I should call his doctor. I'm placed on hold until a pleasant voice offers her sympathy for my loss and asks how I am doing. Then I'm transferred to Dr. Blakely and although we've never met, he sounds cooperative until I ask about Art's prescriptions. "The police have called, Mrs. Finlay, and I told them what I could about the Lipitor and the atenolol. I don't know of any other prescription drugs he might have been using. If he was, I didn't prescribe them."

"He never spoke to you about being depressed?"

"I have no note of that. I certainly did not offer medication for anything other than high blood pressure and cholesterol. The records from his former doctor indicate only Lipitor. Is there anything else?"

"Do you even remember my husband, Dr. Blakely?"

"I have many patients. His file says he was in several months ago. I have a vague memory of an older man who seemed impatient and perhaps tense. Our meeting lasted about fifteen minutes."

"How do you know? About the fifteen minutes?"

"All of my appointments are scheduled for that amount of time."

"And no barbiturates, Valium?"

"No. I note what I prescribe, Mrs. Finlay. No psychotropic drugs or sedatives."

"So how did he renew his prescriptions?"

"Mr. Finlay wasn't due for a checkup for three months. My patients fill prescriptions between checkups by phone with the pharmacist. And now, I need to get on to my next appointment."

I hang up. Dr. Blakely apparently does not like to be suspected of any part in a questionable death. "I feel the same way," I say out loud as I pick up the matchbook covers. "I've got to get some air." I sound a lot like my dead husband as he left the house to walk and maybe hummed "You Are My Sunshine." Perhaps the cardboard scraps of matchbook covers will lead me to where Art went to get his air. I grab my red jacket and go to the car.

The Metrobar hunkers in the midst of blocks of low-lying warehouses. The only thing metro about it is its neon sign flashing against the dusky evening air. When I walk toward the door I can see, through a gray cloud rising from the gaggle of smokers at the entrance, a man behind the bar, two or three people leaning over it. The smell of the place, cigarettes, beer, the peanut shells crunching under my shoes, makes me want to turn around, get back in the car, retreat from this weird mission.

And I wish I'd dressed for the part. A female my age, about to hoist herself onto a bar stool, should have red lips and ginger hair and stretch jeans and a sequined black jacket. At least that's what the only other old woman is wearing, her elbows on the counter, chuckling through smoker's gurgles at the bartender. "You're right, Sam. They shoot horses, don't they?"

How Jane Fonda has gotten into the conversation might be a mystery to anyone listening, anyone under sixty. They've been talking about getting old, the woman and the bartender, and she is a little drunk, in the sloppy way old women relive what they once knew of sex, youth, desire.

"I'm not there yet," she turns, sends a dismissing glance my way. "Still functioning, if you know what I mean. Not like some people." She turns her back to me, and flashes what I now see are inch-long lashes at the bartender. After I test a sticky stool, yes, it's stable, I pull myself onto it, and the ginger-haired woman glances over her shoulder and sizes me up. "I don't believe I know you."

One set of eyelashes is askew, making the woman look cockeyed and a bit crazy.

I adjust my buttocks and find myself becoming someone else. I wink at a man with a tattoo on his neck and a huge round thing in his earlobe, and I say, "I'll have what she's having," a line I know I've heard somewhere. I rest my forearms on the bar so that my boobs overlap them and puff up, filling the V-neck of my T-shirt.

"I'm Edith," I say to the woman next to me. "Can I buy you a beer or something?"

"Mildred." Mildred seems in a quandary. Beer or bartenders? Beer wins out, and she turns on her stool and raises her glass. "Sure. I'm all for new friends."

I know I'm not much of a threat to Mildred, plain, gray, un-eye-lashed as I am, simply a source of refreshments. But maybe Mildred will be helpful. "Come here often?" I ask, and as soon as I say it, I remember the cartoon of the old guy asking the bargirl, "Do I come here often?"

I'm not breathing right, nerves a spinning Rolodex of silly jokes. Unleashed. I could be out of my mind, for real. The beer in front of me may calm me down a little.

Mildred shrugs. "Kind of like family, you know?'

I look around.

The tattooed man setting up glasses, the white-bearded geezer at the end of the bar looking at us over his inflamed cheeks, the three twenty-somethings, giggling into their pink drinks and watching the door are all expecting something or someone, just as I am.

I sip my beer and set the glass down on its paper napkin. "Do you know Art?" I ask. I hope I sound only curious, not desperate.

"Art?" Mildred shrugs. "Don't recall him." She grins. "Did you lose him?"

"In a way, I guess. Somebody I used to know. I heard he hung out here sometimes." I hear myself mimicking Mildred's slur.

Mildred's eyelashes flap. "Know an Art, Billy?"

The bartender stops wiping the glasses and looks at me. "Know a couple of them."

"Older guy, a little overweight, scar on his cheek, probably came in late at night, maybe once a week or so." I remember his midnight breath. "Drank bourbon."

"Yeah, maybe. That Art. Scar. Haven't seen him lately. You a friend?"

"Kind of. Kind of his wife, you know?" I pull out a photo I've kept in my wallet for ten years for some unknown reason, certainly not so that I wouldn't forget him.

Billy squints, seems to accept what I've just admitted. "Yeah. Doesn't drink too much, just enough to get home."

"What did he talk about?"

"Like most old guys, just 'I should have's' and 'why didn't I's?' Oh, yeah, for him it is a gas station he could have made a fortune with...you know how they talk."

"If only..."

Billy keeps wiping the counter. "They all have if only's."

"If only I hadn't gotten pregnant..." I suggest.

"Yeah, they all talk about stuff like that. Wife pregnant, investment gone south, a book that would have made a million only someone else wrote it first—you know, times you turn something down for good reasons, only it turns out the good reasons aren't that good."

"So did Art talk about a lot of turned-down good chances?"

"Not much. But that's the song I hear on this side of the bar. Every night, just old guys regretting."

"Many nights? He came in here?"

"Every once in a while, kind of late, like he'd been somewhere else before."

"Like?"

"I can't say."

"A woman?"

"Just somewhere else, to close the night. He is a quiet guy, lots on his mind. He mostly just drinks, listens, leaves."

The nights he had to get some air. I was usually asleep when he crawled into bed. Sometimes in the mornings his pillow smelled of alcohol and smoke and one night, oranges. I look at the tables behind me. No ashtrays on the tables. No oranges.

"Is he okay?" The bartender takes my glass. "Another?"

I shake my head to both questions. "He had matches from this place in his pocket."

Billy points to a basket near the door. The matchbooks piled in it have overflowed onto the peanut shells on the floor. "I put it there to encourage people to take their cigarettes outside. We get lots of complaints from nonsmokers."

"Art's dead," I say as I push myself off the stool and stand up, crunching.

Billy nods, keeps wiping the glasses in front of him.

Beside me Mildred gives a little moan. "My husband, too. Five years ago. Dropped dead on a street corner..." Having found a kindred soul, she would have gone on, but I head toward the basket. Matchbooks and a messy path lead out through the door onto the sidewalk to somewhere else. Where is the car? I glance left and right, choose right for no good reason except I always choose right when I don't know which way to go. Art used to grab my arm as the department store elevator door opened and guide me toward the exit. On my own, I'd often end up at a makeup counter or plowing through tables of sale underwear before I found my way out of Meier & Frank's. Art always knew where he was going. I make a U-turn. See my car ahead. I should have gone left.

As I pass the bar, Mildred appears in front of me, calls, "Oh, hi!" She moves to my side. "I want to talk to you. About having a husband die. Okay?"

I am too startled to tell the woman to go away. Mildred bumps against me as she sways. She reaches for my arm.

"I tried to figure out what he was doing on that street corner in the first place. In the heart of Chinatown, kitty-corner from a Chinese social club. Herb didn't even like Chinese food. Then I noticed the porn shop a half block away, Fantasy Land. And it all clicked. The Visa charges, the coming home late from work, the scummy books I later find hidden on the bookshelf behind the ones he hadn't read—you know, history of this, biography of that. Discovered all that after he died. You're looking for answers, too, aren't you?" Mildred stops at the curb. "Be careful. You may not like what you find."

I want the woman to let go of my sleeve. I also wish I could straighten that un-glued set of eyelashes. "I'm not sure what you're saying. My husband died in our bed. We had few secrets from each other." I pull away from her hand. "I just need..."

"Please don't say closure. It doesn't work that way." Her grip tightens. "I went into Fantasy Land, you know, looked at videos, looked at foreign objects and wondered how they were used, tried to imagine Herb in this place, maybe fingering the same plastic cocks I picked up. And I could imagine it. And I still do. I can still see my husband getting his rocks off in a dark cubicle sticky with cum. I see him standing at that counter, maybe getting hard, wishing for someone." Tears are leaving trails down Mildred's rouged cheeks, and she lets go of my coat and takes a tissue from her pocket, wipes her nose, dabs at the corners of her eyes, dislodges the drifting strand of eyelashes and plucks it from her eyelid. Feels for the other set. "Someone not me. I see him every night until I fall asleep."

I can't think of anything to say, so I surprise myself by hugging her with one arm. I smell beer and I step away before the hug is returned. "You're tired," I say. "It's time to go home."

Mildred stuffs the tissue, now wrapped around both rows of eyelashes, back into her pocket, her eyes plain, empty. "Yeah. Thanks for listening." I watch as the ginger-haired woman straightens her shoulders, walks unsteadily away from me down the cracked sidewalk.

6

Mildred's Kleenex had been white, not pink.

I sit at the desk, the contents of the WHY? envelope again spread in front of me. I know only one thing for sure, that Art had spent some hours in a tavern and sometimes talked to the barman. That depressed white-bearded man on the end stool convinced me of the truth of the scene. Art, down in the mouth, as usual not talking much, fit right in.

Except for the few times over the years when he did talk to me, when I could feel a change in his climate, an emotional barometer rising, showing a high-pressure front coming in, widening his eyes, words flowing out of him. "How about this?" he asked one night, his newspaper finished and folded in his lap. "Us buying a fishing boat, living on the coast, getting rich on crabs selling for two bucks a pound? We'd only work during the R months, have time to travel somewhere warm." I didn't say much, just wondered how far this dream would soar before it burst in the chill of reality, like the others. He didn't mention a fishing boat again.

The question now, as I poke through the bits of debris in front of me, is where did that idea, and a few others over the years, come from? I don't know. Didn't back then either.

It wasn't that Art never dreamed. He, at the beginning, had dreams and he shared them with me. Right after we got married, his first dream was to buy the gas station he worked at. The old owner wasn't about to spend a lot of time getting dirty, and he let Art do most of the changing of oil, cleaning windshields, pumping gas, replacing windshield wipers and repairing flats. Mr. Jensen sat behind the cash register, counting out bills, handing back change, and sometimes offering credit to friends, the transactions recorded on a pad with carbon copies for the borrowers. On slow days, he would walk over to the café for a cup of coffee, and if he were feeling generous, he'd bring back a donut to Art.

The two men had a relationship based on need: each needed the other despite the fact that Mr. Jensen was a member of St. Rose's, and Art had been confirmed in Trinity Lutheran church two blocks farther on. They didn't talk religion, but sometimes the old man hinted that he might like to retire, relax at his cabin on Fishhook Lake. So Art started saving money, socking it away a little at a time, despite the costs of having a son and a wife.

Then one day a black De Soto pulled in under the station's canopy. Two men got out, told Art, "Fill'er up" and went around the corner to use the restroom. When they came back, Art was washing the windshield. "Three dollars, fifteen cents," he told them, rag in one hand, receipt in the other.

"'Fraid not. Take us inside to the cash register." One of them tucked his hand into a bulging pocket.

Mr. Jensen had gone down to the café, and Art was alone. He led the men inside, trying to figure out what to do. Later, he explained that all he could come up with was the tire iron leaning against the doorframe. As he passed it, he grabbed the awkward thing and swung it at the first man. He missed. Afterward, he had only a vague memory of the metal rod heading in his direction.

When Mr. Jensen returned, a maple bar stored in a paper bag for the afternoon, he found Art bleeding and unconscious, and the till empty. He called the police, who took Art to the hospital for stitches in his cheek. He was lucky that day, but the next day Mr. Jensen fired Art.

"He thought I could have saved the money," Art said as he nursed a beer that evening, black strings from fifteen stitches waving on his cheek. "It's over," he added. "We need to get out of here, find somewhere else, out West, maybe in Oregon. I heard from Tony that the shipyards might be still hiring."

So we left, following a shipyard dream. except the war had ended, and the only ship he worked on was one being torn apart in a ship scrapping yard. That yard closed too. The next dream involved plastic, a new postwar miracle. Someone told Art that a local factory was making plastic containers with lids for all kinds of stuff, mostly food, and the machinery did it all. All a worker had to do was to make sure the machines kept going, and the best part was that the owner wanted to move to California and was looking for a good man to take over, once he'd gotten trained. The problem was, after two weeks Art began coughing up green goop, couldn't catch his breath, red eyes watering. After three weeks of hacking, he took a day off and went to a doctor who told him the plastic fumes were making him asthmatic. He'd have to quit or he'd get sicker, maybe die.

Art's dreams always ended before they ever took hold. The gas station dream, the shipyard dream, the plastic factory dream, the RV-around-the-country dream, and who knows what else. He took a job as a mailman in a nearby suburb, the only dream that involved a government retirement fund. That dream came true.

I don't recall having any dreams of my own. Empty of dreams, for a long time. Uncomfortable thoughts like this must be part of mourning, if that's what I'm doing.

NEVER TOO LATE

I need to get busy, stop making myself feel so unexpectedly sad. I pick up another pocket clue. This matchbook
advertises Boo's Soul, Louisiana BBQ. I'd read about this
place somewhere, probably in the Oregonian's reviews.
Sounds black, in the north part of town. I haven't had a
need to go into that area much, except for the time I got
lost going over the wrong bridge and had to stop and ask a
woman waiting to cross the street the way to where I was
going. She was pleasant, sent me on in the right direction.

I decide I'll go to this Boo's for a drink or something.
However, I don't know how to get to Boo's. I find the ad
and trace the route on a map from the glove box in the car.

At each corner, I am honked at. My car is obviously
moving too slowly. Finally I see the sign and a parking spot
at the same time. The restaurant's windows shine yellow in
the gray afternoon. I can smell the barbecued ribs and the
smoke that pours out of the black drum next to the front
door. Art came here? Art, who wouldn't eat anything that
required his fingers to bring the food to his mouth, even
chicken wings? I get out of my car, am careful to lock the
doors, squint through the windows of the restaurant. I'm not
the only white person. I lower my shoulders, take a breath.
As I walk in, a woman, her cheerful voice reassuring me,
asks if I have come for dinner. That's when I notice the long
bar off to my right, lined with active-eyed men and smiling
women. I'd be better off on the food side of the place.

"Yes, dinner, please."

I'm led through a labyrinth of wooden tables and smiling people wiping their lips with wads of paper napkins. The heady smell of barbeque sauce is as thick as the laughter around me. We arrive at a table in a far corner, next to what I am sure is the restroom, its door swinging in my direction. "Is there another?" I ask, and the waitress tells me she has a table in the bar. "That's fine." I will be drowned by a booming rhythmic beat that I'm assuming must be music. Better than by a flushing toilet.

When I sit down, several men glance over their shoulders at me and then go back to their drinks. I realize I should have brought a book or something to read. Instead I find a pen in my pocket and unfold the paper napkin in front of me, glad to have something to turn my eyes to.

I write. In this foreign place I may uncover a clue to a mystery I never felt, did not grasp, some scrap of truth that will lead me to a man I never met.

Poetic, I think, and I am pleased with my words. I fold the napkin, tuck it into my pocket, and discover the waitress standing at my elbow.

"Oh." I haven't even looked at the menu. "Which ribs do you like best?"

She points to the third item on the handwritten list. "My favorite," she says, and I suspect she says this to every clueless white person who asks.

"Okay. And a glass of dry white wine."

"We've got chablis. That's pretty dry. Or we've got mer-lot. Red. And we've got different beers. Right here." She points to the menu.

"Beer." I can't remember what kind Mildred and I drank. "Something pale yellow."

I look around the room as the waitress inserts her pad behind her belt and makes her way to the bar. A man turns on his stool and dips his head at me. My new buddy Mildred would have batted her eyelashes at him. I feel my cheeks heat up. I look down at the pen beside my plate and wish I hadn't put away the napkin.

"That gentleman just bought you this beer." The wait-ress is back. I notice her nametag, MiKaela, as she settles a glass in front of me.

"Man?" But I know which man. Now he's wagging a fin-ger at me.

By the time the ribs arrive, our eyes have met enough times to warn me that he'll make his way to the empty chair beside me. I eat quickly. And when I push my plate away, finished, he is sitting across from me.

He's very attractive. I surprise myself. I've not often al-lowed myself to consider a black man's looks. His gray hair, clipped close to his scalp, frames smooth, brown cheeks, his green eyes seem lit from inside.

"Don't see many women like you here."

"Old white women?"

"Handsome white women," he answers. "My-age women."

An ancient, long-forgotten stirring flutters deep in my body. "I'm Edith," I decide to admit.

"I'm Seth. And you are a handsome woman, Edith. A pleasure to sit by."

No one has ever told me I am handsome. Handsome isn't sexy. Handsome is...strong. Or forthright. Or determined. Well, I can be determined. I take a deep breath, douse the churn of adrenaline or hormones, whatever, and get to work. "I wonder if you knew my husband," I say. My finger rubs against my wedding ring. Force of habit, still wearing it. Probably can't get it past my knuckle without lotion.

"Maybe. Name?"

"Art Finlay. He came here once in a while, I'm pretty sure."

"And you are looking for him?"

"He's dead. And yes, I'm looking for him. Tall, belly, balding dark hair, scar on his left cheek, not social, used to visit at least one bar regularly, and maybe this place." I take out the matchbook cover, tap on it as if it will open, reveal the secret.

"Don't believe I know him. Maybe MiKaela?" He motions to the waitress, and she makes her way to us. Her hand brushes the row of braids at her temple and then touches on the man's shoulder, the gesture easy and familiar.

"What's up, Seth?"

"This here nice woman is looking to find out if her husband came here once in a while. She's trying to find out...about his movements. Let's see if we can help her a little. What's his name, Edith?"

"Art. Six feet, close to two fifty, roundish in that way that old guys get." I glance at Seth. "Some guys. Fringe of dark hair."

"Black man?" MiKaela checks with Seth; he nods an okay. I am realizing the advantages of being a harmless-looking old woman, handsome as she may be. I should join the CIA, maybe.

"No, don't remember him." MiKaela, busy serving up ribs for hours every night, will never remember a nondescript, aging white guy who probably frowned at his ribs as he scraped the meat off them with a fork and knife, the unsteady fork held in his left hand as if he'd been raised in a foreign country, the knife like a scalpel. "One thing about him," I add. "A small scar here." I touch my cheek. "And his hands shook when he held something. Especially his left hand. Got worse as he got older. Spilled coffee sometimes and used a spoon a lot."

"We get that sometimes. One lady comes in alone and sits in that table you didn't like, facing the wall. We help her get her napkin tucked in around her neck, another one for her lap. Must be hard..."

Then I remember the old photo, find it in my purse, and hand it to the waitress.

"Yeah, a guy who looks a little like this came in once in a while, like you describe. Spilled his drink into his lap one night, got mad, wouldn't let me help him, just ordered another drink. That could've been who you're looking for."

I can picture it. "Was he with someone? When he came in?" Or later, like myself sitting here with a stranger named Seth.

"He said he was meeting someone. I figured that's why he got so mad over his wet pants. It was a while ago, more than a month or so ago." MiKaela shifts the dishes in her hands and heads toward the kitchen.

"Well, that's that." I drain the last of the beer, crush a pile of paper napkins after I wipe my hands, and push back my chair. "At least I know he came here once, maybe more. I just don't know why. Art didn't like ribs." The plate in front of me is stacked with clean bones. I twist and reach for my coat hanging on the back of my chair. "Thanks for the beer, Seth."

"He did meet someone here." Seth's words stop my arm halfway into its sleeve, leave me hanging as I wait for what's coming next. "I remember that night. I was about to leave. Your husband, his angry voice, you know, attracted my attention. And I wasn't the only one looking and others' attention."

Seth stretches an arm across my shoulders, helps straighten my coat.

"He met a young woman. They didn't talk very much, just ate. She left before he did. She was lovely, black, with hair that sprang in corkscrews around her face, onto her shoulders. She looked like a schoolgirl out with her father, a little bored, hungry. I noticed her because she reminded me of someone I once knew."

"A whore? The schoolgirl, that is?"

"No, but they did some business—an envelope passed between them before she left." Seth leans back in his chair. "So, have you found your husband?"

His voice makes my stomach do that thing again, but it could have been the ribs.

I stand and survey the first man who has ever told me I am handsome. "Thank you, Seth. Piece of him, maybe." Then, without warning, my hand brings out the pen in my pocket, tears a piece off the napkin, writes my name and phone number. "In case you remember anything else."

He takes the scrap, folds it, slips it into his jacket pocket. "Goodnight, handsome lady. It's Seth Benjamin." He grins at me. At me.

7

"So, how are you, Edith? I tried to call last night, but you weren't home." Kathleen's question sounds like an accusation.

"I went out for a while," I say. None of your business, I'd like to add. "Had ribs, honey-hot ribs. Ever have them?" I'm brushing my hair, looking into the bathroom mirror again, listening to the phone with one hand and ear, and trying to see a handsome woman. Her neck isn't too bad, especially when she raises her head; her hair is longer than usual, since she has not visited the Love Yourself salon for a couple of months. Curls wind under her ears, into her collar.

NEVER TOO LATE

When did I decide I had to keep it short, old-lady short? About the time I stopped wearing a bra, I guess. No good news down there.

"Hello? Are you still there?"

"Yes. Just preoccupied with my toilette." I've read that phrase somewhere. It doesn't stop Kathleen for a second.

"Edith. You sound...strange. Should I come by, bring a couple of blueberry scones from the bakery?" She doesn't wait for an answer. "Yes, I will. Put the pot on. I'll be there in ten minutes. Can't wait to hear about the ribs." The ribs are on my mind, too. Not the ribs but the word that accompanied them. Handsome. Not quite, my mirror answers.

I decide. It's time to resurrect myself, give the dead man a rest. I'll get a haircut, but it will be a spiky, held together with "product," like Marie tried to describe an appointment or two ago, and the hair will be a pale blond. I'll need to do something about pinking up my cheeks, too, and deal with the dark circles I can see when I take off my glasses and get close to the mirror. And of course, the boobs.

When the doorbell rings, the coffee is ready, and so am I. Ready for whatever this almost-relative of mine is about to try to do for me. I can't relate to her do-for-others kind of outlook. Not anymore, at least. I'd started out that way, of course: doing, doing, doing, not noticing in the process that no one was doing for me. Not when I needed it, anyway. That thought makes me hesitate a moment, my hand reaching out at the sound of the bell, an almost-forgotten scene inserting itself between my fingers and the doorknob.

At one point a month after Brian was born, I considered smothering him. I had a plan involving the new mattress and feather pillows and a heavy quilt with which I would suffocate him and then myself, a thought not appropriate at the moment because the pain in my breasts was keeping me from doing anything more than holding my son across my knees, aiming a tender a teat at him. My terribly angry son kept pushing away from me as if I were offering him cyanide. Perhaps I was, my milk contaminated by whatever was going on inside me. He howled for his real mother, the warm, milky one he'd gotten used to, but any touch on my nipples—his lips, my own fingers—sent excruciating daggers through my body. "Latch on, damn it!" I hissed as I squeezed his hot, red cheeks. We were huddled under heavy bedclothes, it was 2 a.m., and I couldn't take motherhood a moment longer.

My wails joined Brian's, and Art, even then his back facing me, turned over and mumbled, "Jesus Christ, can't you shut him up? I have to go to work in three hours." He grabbed a blanket and lurched into the front room and the sofa there.

That scene was what saved Brian. And maybe me. The problem wasn't about having a baby, really. It was about having a husband.

NEVER TOO LATE

My doctor gave me a pill, his nurse showed me how to pump milk, and I bought a bottle with a nipple Brian liked more than mine after I poked a bigger hole in the rubber with a hot needle. The pain in my breasts subsided. Brian began sleeping through the night. I still woke up, though, and lay listening to the snores of the man to whom I'd committed my life in a careless moment, and with whom I had quickly fallen out of love. Those nights, if I hadn't had a sleeping baby in the next room, I might have run away. For Brian's sake, I kept on being the Doer who spent her hours doing for a thankless husband because of love for her son. And Brian turned out to be a perfect child, happy, eager to learn, play with his trucks, turn pages of the picture books we read together, his squeals of laughter offering me asylum from the war between his parents.

I'm not sure when I stopped the doing. Much later. Probably just before Brian got married, when I suggested we buy a new sofa and rug for the wedding events. "We can have the rehearsal party here. I'll cook, and we'll save money that way. We really need to spruce up the house anyway."

Art leaped so quickly I didn't have time to back away. "We don't have to spruce up anything," he growled, his fingers biting into my wrist. His face drew close and I could see into his black pupils and the narrow rim of blue containing them. "You'll cook the dinner if we have to have it, but the money for it comes from your budget, not my pocket. Only a few coins rattle in that pocket at the end of every month."

I yanked my arm away, rubbed what would be bruises the next day. Thirty years of bruises, a few physical, most emotional, joined forces in a declaration of independence, and I hissed, "I'm sick of hearing about your empty pockets. And if you touch me like that one more time, I swear I will leave you." I didn't know where the words, the courage to say them, came from. But I wasn't finished. "Right now, I will be helping Brian address his part of these."

I gathered the wedding invitations, made a neat pile. "And I'll sit right here and make out a menu for his party." I turned my back to him. "And you will find the money somewhere to pay for it." My words still ringing in my head, in the air, against the walls, I could feel Art's footsteps shaking the floorboards as he left the house.

That time I did say no and meant it. And things did change. Art paid the extra grocery bills. He never touched me again, in anger or in love. Only occasionally in lust. I found my new bitchy voice, made lists, new demands: his clothes left on the floor of the closet, his loud TV, the skimpy money in the envelope. Art retreated further from me, more silent than ever. That suited me just fine. Most of the time, at least.

I open the door. "Hi, Mom. I just wanted to check in on you." Kathleen holds out the bag of scones. "And to have a cup of coffee. Hope you have time?"

Mom. Kathleen calls me that when she has something on her mind and is looking for a way into me. I know I'm being cynical, a condition that is hanging on even after its source is dead. "Of course." I give my daughter-in-law a breeze of a kiss on the temple, take her jacket, and lay it on the back of a chair.

In the kitchen Kathleen unloads the scones on a plate, and looks for paper napkins. I point at the napkin drawer and pour the coffee. "Let's sit at the table," she says. "Gets a little sun in the morning."

We both break our pastries in half, and then Kathleen sets hers beside her cup, sends her you-can-trust-me look at me. "I'm here because we're worried that you are unhappy, maybe making yourself even more unhappy by going through Art's pockets, perhaps even making some decisions that don't need to be made yet, like selling the house?" Her lips settle into a lipsticked question mark.

"We? You and my son?" I will not respond to this determined mouth, this intrusive woman. "If Brian is worried, why isn't he here?" I scoot my chair back, ready to stand up when she reaches across the table, her hand inches from mine.

"No, Edith, not so much we. Me. I'm worried. About you, not the house, about your—" She hesitates, trying, maybe, to find a word that won't send me out of the room. "—about your need to find pieces of Art, to maybe reconstruct him, to understand him better now than when he was alive." Her hand has slipped away; her eyes unblinkingly fervent. "It seems like fruitless scavenging, not knowing what you are looking for, unhappy when you don't find it. What good will it do? You can't change the past, and you have a future to look forward to."

I hate her not-knowing guesses. "The pockets are not making me unhappy." Confused, but not unhappy. And how can she, the perfect wife and mother, judge about unhappiness anyway? "And I'm not going to sell the house soon. Where'd you get that idea?" Brian and my new financial advisor must have been talking. "Why is my son checking up on me? Herbert Smith told me that it is my right to use Art's retirement fund, to sell the house, whatever, in any way that I want."

"Yes." Kathleen nods as if she agrees; a little smile creeps back towards me. "It's just that you don't have to decide anything for a while, until you are really ready. Art's death took all of us by surprise, you especially."

"Actually, not. I imagined Art dead a number of times." I take a bite of scone and wash it down with coffee. "Is that a terrible thing to say?" I enjoy the look on Kathleen's face that says it is. "Don't you ever try to imagine what life would be like without Brian? Most wives do, I'm pretty sure. And they do it more often when they don't love their husbands."

"You can't mean that. You were married for almost fifty years."

"Does that make a difference?"

"Love changes. I know that, after twenty years. But it still is there, under all of the other layers of stuff. Isn't it?" She looks down, seems to be seeking something in her cup as if it holds the answer.

Something about Kathleen's voice makes me take a good look at the woman across the table from me. Tears?

"What?" I ask.

A pale, ringed hand covers her brow and eyes. I have to lean forward to hear what she is saying. "This is so bad. One is not supposed to complain about her husband to that man's mother, is she?"

I sit back, pull off another corner of scone. What could she possibly have to complain about? That he works too hard? Is too stressed out to go along with her orderliness? Doesn't have time to help with the kids? All part of building a successful business, isn't it? I wouldn't know, of course, but I assume supporting Brian's career is part of her contract with him, that she signed on as his helpmeet, just as I did, back when that word was part of the marriage vows. Most women, I imagine, feel frustrated in that role once in a while. But look what she's gotten—children, a great house, a fine man to live with. She must have someone other than her mother-in-law to dump on.

But I've never seen my competent daughter-in-law teeter into tears before. I'm curious. "Try me."

Kathleen clears her throat, moves away from the rays of sun coming in from the garden. "I suspect that Brian is seeing someone." At these words, tears escape, leak along her nose. "Sometimes he comes home late."

Now it is I who can barely speak. "And?"

"I peeked at the calendar in his planner. He's blocked off time for the past few weeks, with just the initial P written in." She closes her eyes. "I shouldn't be telling you this."

"No, probably not." This is my perfect son we're talking about. There must be a logical explanation.

Kathleen shifts in her chair, reaches for her cup, doesn't pick it up, wipes a finger across a flooded cheek. "I'm too embarrassed to tell him I read his calendar, that I don't trust him." She hesitates. "This must be hard for you, Edith. You and Brian are so close."

If our roles were reversed, she'd be telling me what to do right now. Is that what she wants? I can do that. I could say, "You have to talk to Brian, not me. I'm sure he has an explanation. Maybe he has dentist appointments or something, a dentist whose name begins with P." I shake my head. Too easy. I'm the wrong person for this. I cannot accept what she is implying. "I'm no good at helping people, Kathleen. Especially when it concerns my son."

She stands, walks into the living room and I'm off the hook.

"I came to ask if I could help you, Edith, and instead I've made you angry. Please don't tell Brian about this. I'll figure out what I should do." At the front door, Kathleen slips into her jacket. "I was going to tell you that sometimes I can smell her on him. Would that have made a difference?"

Shit.

8

A surge of energy fired by my disappointment in Brian has
led to a day of dumping everything connected to his father
into the back of the car and leaving Art at Goodwill. Goodwill doesn't take old photos or scraps of pocket papers, so
those leftovers are waiting in wastebaskets in the front hall.
However, I don't feel better despite the purging. I make my
way to my new light-blue lounger and settle back to try to
decide what to do.

Nothing. I can do nothing about my son's apparent decision to be unfaithful. Because I can't make myself believe
what she has told me, I can do nothing to ease Kathleen's
pain. In fact, I keep wanting to blame her. Is she imagining
this? Paranoid? A bit unhinged? I have been aware that at

times Brian has been unhappy at work, but who isn't? He has confessed to me, once or twice, disappointment with the way his life is going, or is not going: his future, his marriage, and once, his relationship with his father. All normal disappointments, if I can judge by the advice column I read daily in the newspaper. However, if he is indeed heading into the arms of another woman, coming home carrying her scent, any apron strings still tying me to Brian are being stretched way too far.

The manila WHY? envelope sticking out of the wastebasket catches my eye. His father went out for some air. Why not Brian?

Because he won't betray me.

At that thought, I struggle out of the chair and head for the kitchen. "I need a drink of something. I'm going nuts," I say to the pantry door. I find a bottle with an inch of bourbon in it, pour it in a glass, add an ice cube and, having second thoughts about what I'm doing, add a little water.

How can I believe that a son's having a lover betrays his mother? Nuts. Absolutely. I lift the glass again, pause. Maybe it is my hope for him that is betrayed, the happy-ever-after-hope. Not a betrayal of the mother, though. Really, only his wife. Of course, his wife. I finish my drink, wash out the glass, go to the desk, and call her. I need to find out more--about betrayal and truth.

Kathleen and I meet at a small restaurant on a side street in the center of town. My daughter-in-law slides onto her chair with a small sigh, meeting my eyes only for a moment.

"I am here to listen, Kathleen. I wasn't ready before. I am now."

Kathleen opens her menu. I tell myself to wait.

"Thank you. I'm sorry I dumped on you the other day. I feel better now."

No, you don't, I think as she turns a page, doesn't look up at me. "I'm glad if you do." I open at my own menu. "I wish I could say as much." Again I wait, pretending to be trying to make a choice.

Kathleen's head lifts. 'What do you mean? Is something wrong? Besides Art's dying, of course."

"It's not about his being dead." I pause on purpose, know I need to do this, to go on. "I've discovered what seems to be Art's secret life while he was alive. His life for a while, anyway. I won't bother you with it. Let's order." I look for our waitress, but Kathleen shakes her head.

"What secret life?"

I have never had many friends. The three women that I still consider best friends, even though the years have changed what best means, became intimates when, as young women, we shared our worries about our mothering, our doubts about our marriages, our uneasiness about who we were becoming or not becoming. Over coffee, usually, while our children played a room away. This sharing was mutual. One day Eleanor would be in a funk. Sherry's turn came the day she felt so awful she wanted to hide in a closet, and might have if it hadn't been her turn to have the klatch at her house that morning. Lynne, quiet, listening, commenting only on what the others were saying, didn't share much until the day she walked in and collapsed over the plate of cookies and revealed that Tim had attempted suicide the night before. Through those ten or so years, the years our children shared schools and infectious diseases, we didn't see our morning coffees as complaining, only as a way of examining our days, looking for advice or just being listened to. It had all started with one of us opening up. It ended when we moved onto new houses, husbands, lives.

I take a deep breath, about to try to share in that same way with my daughter-in-law. Intimacy breeds intimacy, a truth I discovered over coffee years ago.

"You know, I'm sure, that my marriage was not joyful. I don't remember a day of joy, in fact, although I suspect there were a few. I often wondered what life would have been like for me had I not become pregnant, but less so when I realized that Brian gave me the love his father could not. So we marched on, getting older, watching Brian grow up, get his own family. I kept a house and its meals as if I would always be a mother and a wife. Art went to work. Then he retired and our roles bottomed out. What I didn't realize was that Art's life was empty, as empty as mine. After he died, I found remnants of what he had tried to do to fill the emptiness. You know a little about my snooping into his pockets, his calendar, his desk."

The waitress arrives and we both order the first salad on the menu. "And two glasses of white, dry wine," I add.

Then I continue, not sure where I am going. "I've found out that Art's leaving the house at night led him to a bar where he sat and talked with the bartender, to a restaurant where he had a late supper with a young black girl with curly hair, eating ribs that he wouldn't ever let me cook. I don't know where his pockets will take me next. Wherever it is, it can't make me feel any worse about our marriage than I do right now. How could I not have known?" I realize I'm being a little dramatic, as I add, "I've never understood men." This sentence comes straight from my friend thirty-some years ago, coffee the lubricant then, not the too-oaky chardonnay the woman has placed in front of us.

"Damn," Kathleen sighs. "Neither do I." She sips at her wine, raises her eyebrows, eyes wide. It's her turn. "I thought I was a perfect wife. I keep a good house, have raised mostly good kids, have learned to cook everything " She hesitates, apparently decides to say it. "I get myself ready for sex every night. You know what I mean."

I'm not sure I do.

"So here I am, reading a book, waiting for Brian to come home from an increasing number of night meetings, cleaned up, diaphragm at the ready, and when he walks in, I notice it. I told you. Her smell. And he falls into bed. 'Too hard a day,' he says, 'Good night, honey, next time,' and he rolls over asleep."

"Sex smell?" Faint memories of such a smell, my own, inspire me to ask.

"Sort of, perfumish. A little flowery with a hint of citrus.

Trust this perfectionist to have a perfect nose. Must be annoying at times, especially when the scent is leaking from the skin of a husband. Actually, I am remembering that a similar scent lurked under Art's bourbon breath one night. But this isn't the time to go there. Later. I pull myself back to Kathleen's words. "How long has this lateness been going on?"

"A couple of months, I guess." The salads have arrived, spinach with beets and feta. Kathleen stabs a fork into a maroon ball, which flies onto the table, rolls off to the floor. "I can't even eat anymore!" She dabs at her eyes with her napkin. "Mom, I'm a mess."

So this is what it must be like to have a daughter, an almost-perfect daughter except when she's falling apart. So this is what it might be like being a mother to such a daughter. All I can do at that moment is reach out with my own napkin and wipe the snot from my daughter's upper lip. "We can figure this out."

Snuffling a little, Kathleen cuts into the next beet, forks a little cheese on the slice, gets it to her mouth. "I love beets," she says.

9

After lunch, Kathleen hesitates as we head for our cars and our separate lives. She stops walking, and my next step brings me so close to her that I see the mascara draining from one corner of her eye. She's crying again.

"What?"

She shakes her head. "I've been so busy working, being a wife, a mother, that I've forgotten what it's like to have someone to share secrets with."

Kathleen's coat sleeve is smudged as she brings her wrist away from her face. "Freshman year in the dorm, maybe. Broken hearts. Late night confessions. Who knew I'd need friends like that twenty-five years later? God..." Her lips tremble as she turns away.

"I haven't talked to my three old friends in a long time," I say to her retreating back. "We haven't needed each other, I guess. I didn't even call them when Art died. I could have talked to you and didn't realize it." I'm struck by that thought. I find myself reaching out, wrapping my arms around the huddle of the woman in front of me. I've never liked hugging. First, that ginger-haired woman at the bar and now my once-difficult daughter-in-law. Hugging may become a habit.

When we separate, blinking away tears, we decide we will help each other unravel the tangles our husbands have created. We will spend a day or so on Art before going on to Brian. Kathleen will let her own mystery simmer for a while, waiting for the next P on her husband's calendar. Eyes finally dry, she reassures me in her old decisive way as we part, "I'm so glad we have found each other."

The next day, the credit card receipts we've emptied out of the bag in front of us capture our attention. Having lived their whole lives in Art's pockets, the thin tissues are folded, smudged, almost unreadable. My daughter-in-law flattens one, squints, dials the number she manages to make out, the phone in speaker mode.

"Hilton Suites," the voice says. "Can I help you?"

"Yes. Where are you?" Kathleen asks, eyeing me. Her eyebrows raise as she mouths at me, Have your ever stayed at a Hilton?

The woman tells her, "Right here in downtown Portland, on Broadway. A great location." Kathleen hangs up.

"Art was never away all night." That's all I can manage to say. "Maybe somebody else?"

"Like he paid for a room for somebody else?"

I try to picture Art in the Hilton. He'd walk out of that ostentatious lobby before he could find the registration counter. No, not Art.

"Let's look at the next receipt." Kathleen is being efficient, but perhaps a little careless, not concerned about the consequences of her thoroughness. I am. What unbelievable place will we be directed to next? She reads the name aloud: "Jake's Crawfish?"

The best seafood restaurant in town. Art could hardly bring to his lips the sole I used to batter up and serve with frozen French fries. Crawfish? The thought makes even me squirm a little. A look must have crossed my face at that thought because Kathleen chuckles. "It's early. But I only have a sitter until six."

I tuck the receipt in my purse and get up. I, for once, know something Kathleen doesn't. My daughter-in-law apparently doesn't read the ads in the Oregonian's entertainment section. "That'll work," I tell her. "Happy hour. Half price drinks. Very popular." I pull on a sweater and head out the door. Kathleen doesn't hesitate, except to reach for the tube of lipstick in her pocket.

We make our way through a suited throng, men and women. The dark wood walls and marble-topped bar shimmer in the low, seductive light, drinkers' voices softened by the low candles in the center of the tables and the slow jazz floating above us. I notice that while Kathleen fits into the generation of people in this room, I am the only gray-haired female. Some of the men have gray hair, of course, and gray eyebrows under which they peer at me and go back into their drinks. I'm getting used to that barroom glance. If I were undecided before, I now know that I will be a blonde very soon.

We find a table, decide on the house's special drink of the day, Long Island iced tea, and I hope that it also has a little alcohol in it because I have suddenly lost the reason I'm there. Kathleen brings me back to the task at hand.

"Take out the credit card receipt. How much was it? For dinner or drinks and how many?"

I can't see in the dim light and hand the paper to Kathleen.

"Shit."

While I don't even notice when I come out with this four-letter word, I've never heard Kathleen use it. "What?"

"Art spent over two hundred dollars on drinks and what looks like three meals. And a tip. A big one."

"Last time we went out it was to Applebee's on a two-for-one offer."

"There's a date on this. About three or four weeks before he died."

"He didn't know two people, at least ones that he wanted to eat with."

"Maybe..."

"Maybe his girlfriend had a girlfriend. Ménage à trois–like." The drink is taking hold now, and I ease into the sweet cloud of music and murmuring. "Maybe my nose isn't as good as yours."

Kathleen glances at me over the lemoned rim of her glass. "That was low, Edith."

I unhook my purse from the back of my chair. "Yes, it was. We should leave before I say anything else hurtful."

The waitress steps toward our table. "Five minutes to the end of Happy Hour. Time to order another Long Island iced tea?" I hear Kathleen say, "Of course, two more for the road, please." Kathleen must be also feeling her drink and is ready to keep feeling it for a while. She fumbles in her pocket for some change. "Phone?" she asks. The waitress points to one sitting on the end of the bar near our table.

Kathleen dials, and I hear her talking to her babysitter. "I've been held up a little, Jennifer. I'll be there a little after seven, if that's okay with you. If the kids are hungry, there's leftover mac and cheese to warm up." She hesitates and adds, "And Cherry Garcia in the freezer. Help yourself."

When she comes back to our table, she asks, "Did that sound like a bribe?"

I nod, and our giggles bring glances from the next table. I don't care. It's not only the Long Island iced tea I'm drinking that makes me giddy, then nostalgic, and maybe even a little sad. It's the fact that I haven't laughed with another woman like this since... "Do you ever meet friends for Happy Hour?"

Kathleen goes solemn. "My best friend is dying of uterine cancer. My other friends have gotten so involved in careers that they don't have time to sit around talking. We get together maybe twice a year, share about work or gossip a little but, no, we don't dig below the top layers like we used to." She pauses. "I suspect you have to trust to do that. We lost that naïve quality as our life became about what we do, not about what we feel."

I understand what she means. "When my friends were mostly housewives, we talked a lot, over morning coffee and cookies. And I guess we trusted each other, except for the few we disliked, the ones who let us know their friendships were only temporary, until their husbands were promoted and they would withdraw to a better neighborhood. But our kids grew up, we grew up, moved, got involved in just staying alive, problems went inward." That thought makes me lift my drink to my lips. "We all probably were a little lonely, but we asked ourselves, who isn't a little lonely? And we just kept going, not caring much, knowing the light at end of the tunnel glowed faintly."

"Then you die? That's it? Edith, that's a horrible way to look at life."

I can see the lamps in the buildings nearby flicker, go dark. Shadows hurry through the dim air as workers head for home. Kathleen's too young to understand getting old. "A few years ago," I say, "one of my coffee klatch friends was found lying in her back yard with a plastic bag tied over her head. She didn't die, but she wished she had from then on. When you are older, death is not so frightening. Art's going apparently wasn't awful for him; he ate gourmet meals until he maybe did himself in and escaped. My friend had the same hope."

Kathleen pushes her glass aside and her narrow fingers capture my knobby ones; the cup of her palm soothes the blue veins above my knuckles. I want to bronze the moment, like those baby shoes years ago: two hands, one old, one young, holding on to each other.

"Mom, you can choose now, about anything that might come next." She squeezes my hand, releases it. "You've never been able to do that."

I raise my glass. "I'm considering becoming a blonde and maybe doing something about my neck." Long Island iced tea is talking, and it sounds so right.

"Shit!"

There, the perfect girl has said it again.

"And we'll go shopping!" Kathleen has raised her voice and an arm and almost spills her drink.

"So why are we here?" Not to get drunk, I'm pretty sure. Someone, I realize, has to get us back on track again and, especially important, out the door. It's close to seven. Cherry Garcia can only do so much when it's bedtime. "Have we discovered anything?"

The server stands at our table again, eyeing the dinner line at the door, letting us know that we have overstayed our welcome unless we are here for dinner.

"Please look at this," Kathleen says to her, smoothing out the wrinkles on a receipt: time of day, number of people? We are...working for a client who found this receipt, and she is needs to know how this piece of paper ended up in her husband's pocket...Tiffany," she adds, glancing the woman's nametag.

Tiffany tucks her pad under her arm and leans closer to the strip of paper and squints at the smudged carbon print.

"Well, it lists four glasses of wine, a mineral water, three surf and turf, two salads, and three desserts. The time here, 9:37 p.m. The server was Becca, at table thirteen, the date, here." She focuses on a smudge. Looks like three guests."

"So is Becca here tonight?" Kathleen opens her wallet, touches the bills filed inside. She's up to something.

Tiffany looks about the room, returns her eyes to the wallet. "Yeah, I'll send her to you."

In a moment, a thin young woman comes to our table, and I'm not sure what to ask her. But Kathleen is on a roll, has a new story. "My mother and I are trying to locate my father, who has disappeared. He's a little ditzy, you know, and he hasn't come home since a few days after this receipt was signed by him."

Becca shakes her head. "That was weeks ago. I hope he's all right. What does he look like?"

"Older, balding, dark hair, a small facial scar, a little ditzy, two other people with him. Maybe two women. He's inclined to be loud when he's angry, which happens often, and—"

I hold out the wrinkled photo. "—his hands tremble when he's holding a glass or a fork. Part of the disease, I guess." How else can I describe this unknowable man I've lived with more than forty years? "He doesn't like most food or loud music."

"Well, that describes half of the old guys who come in here." Becca shakes her head and turns. "Don't remember him."

As a last minute thought occurs to me, I add, "One of the women might have been black with wild, curly ringlets. She's probably too young to drink."

Becca glances back at us, at the photo, and at Kathleen's open wallet. She says, softly, for our ears only, "I remember a table that caused a fuss when I denied a young African-American woman a drink. I thought she must be wearing a

wig, her hair was so springy. She was okay about it, but the
guy she was with wasn't, turned kind of red, and raised his
voice until the other woman calmed him down. Oh, yeah,
and a terrible shirt."

"Hawaiian?"

"Very. We don't get much of that here in Portland, especially on a rainy night."

"And the other woman? Was she black also?

"If she was, I don't remember. She was pretty well put
together, dark suit, gold earrings, silky blouse. I noticed her
clothes because of the contrast between her and him. She
seemed a little embarrassed by his behavior." Becca doesn't
say any more, just looks at Kathleen and waits.

Kathleen slips a bill out of her wallet, gives it to the
waitress, slides another under her Long Island iced tea glass
for Tiffany and then scrapes her chair back and stands. "Got
what we wanted, Edith. Besides, I'm sloshed. Time to go
home."

The best thing about this day is hearing Kathleen say
she is sloshed. The next best thing is the warm palm on my
back as we make our way out the door.

10

The thing that I can't make go away—awake as I am to-night, wide awake, my legs twitchy, and my head cycling, cycling, never stopping—is that idea that maybe my philandering husband committed suicide. One last fuck-you to his family, to me.

Did I really think those words? Fuck you. They have risen easily into my consciousness, as if they've been waiting for the appropriate moment to insert themselves into my vocabulary. I roll over, pull the quilt up to my neck, and squint at the clock. I've been seeing too many Tarentino films. The f-bomb has become ordinary, even necessary now, to describe certain events, like Art's decision to leave me without explanation. Like the time his fingers left bruises on me, only then I didn't have the right words.

Fuck you, I could have said to Art when he squeezed my arm so hard. Fuck you, when I found him dead in my bed. And now that I know for sure he's been with other women, has sat at bars complaining about his life, has eaten $200 dinners without me, I have even more reason to say, Fuck you, Art Finlay.

But that once-taboo word wouldn't have solved anything then, and they certainly don't now. I lie twitching and awake and unable to make sense of it. Who are these women? And why does it bother me so much find out about them? It isn't as if Art and I ever pretended to have a perfect marriage. By the end, we hadn't bothered to pretend anything.

I turn on the light, sit up, and reach for a glass of water. Liquid splashes on my nightgown, wetting my chest, but I can't stop the churning, even with the room lit, a cold river creeping toward my crotch. A thought keeps bubbling up no matter I do to shove it under the surface. Art, lonely, depressed, did something about his dissatisfaction. I felt the same way and continued to fold the laundry and swish out the toilet. Resentments grew like poisonous fungi in a dark place inside myself. He had tried change things. I had not, except to turn into an unlovable shrew imagining a dead husband.

Shit. I get up, tired of pounding on myself as if I were a slab of meat needing tenderizing. What did Kathleen say? Rearrange your thoughts to consider what's next, not what's past. What's next, I decide, is blond. Not a cure for my surf and turf shock this evening, but at least a step towards dealing with the fungi.

"So I'm in your hands. I do not like the battleship-gray mess that has docked on my head," I tell Marie. "I want to be blond. And I want it to be a bit upright, maybe even butch, if that still is a style.

Not my usual closed-eyes haircut. This time I watch, even direct the scissors a couple of times, once the hair is a somewhat-yellow. Perhaps I should have gone ginger, I think. Next time. But yes, of course I want product.

Marie's fingers weave themselves through my new do. I slip on my glasses to see what's happened, and I am astonished. The woman in the mirror has cheekbones. And a smooth forehead. And ears that will support chandeliers.

"Now the bags," I say, satisfied with the first step. I walk across the mall to Faces and in an hour, the bags are not quite gone, but almost. Silver shadows the eyelids; no one will even notice the bags. "I'm not sure I can do this on my own," I confess to Phoenix, my cosmetician.

"Come in whenever you need some encouragement," Phoenix assures me. "Everyone does. Maybe a peel next time. My specialty."

Whatever a peel is, I am going to do it. I've never felt so...what? Not just handsome. Today I feel sexy. Yes, that's it. At this moment, I'd relish bumping into that lovely man, Seth, at Boo's Soul, the one who started me on this trip to becoming all of myself. Along with, to be honest, Art, who helped with his $200 fling at Jake's.

I finally reach Kathleen on the phone, tell her to drop by, so I can show off and find out what's going on with her. Kathleen arrives before picking up the kids after school, and she likes the new Edith. However, I am aware of a roundness that has become an unrelenting girdle around my middle, and I know its name is Snacks. Damn Trader Joes. If I am going to be new from the neck up, I'm going to have to work on the three-quarters of myself below my chin. I ask Kathleen about her health regimen.

"I walk every day, about two miles, then stop for coffee and circle back. It's becoming a ritual. I could meet you at mile two and you could join me for the trip back. Only I walk a little fast, and I do it at 6:30 a.m. Seven o'clock, if you meet up with me?" Her invitation is friendly, not critical. We don't mention Brian. Not enough time, maybe.

"Okay. Seven. I can do this. At least once."

And every Monday, Wednesday, and Friday, I decide after coming home the next morning, blood flowing, legs ready, mind, interestingly enough, only slowly churning, leaving me calm long enough to read the Oregonian and plan my day. Once again, Kathleen and I don't mention Art

or Brian, only how great it feels to get moving early, walking amidst damp fog that swirls though trees beginning to
bud. I suppose we're taking a break from the other fogs we
also are trying to move through.

However, two days later, Kathleen doesn't show up at
our meeting spot. I go out alone, come home, decide to dig
once again into the manila envelope without my sleuth buddy. The Hilton. Why and who? No other clues, only that
credit card receipt. I can do this by myself. I will pretend to
have lost something that night. An earring. An important
earring. I make the call, wait for housecleaning to respond,
for the lost and found drawer to be searched. No earring.
"Please let me know," I say. At the number you have for the
reservation."

"Let me see," a saccharine voice says. "We have 289-4321
as a contact number. Is that correct?"

The number is unfamiliar to me. "Yes," I answer, and I
jot it down on the list of to-do's I've begun. I hang up, and
when I dial the number, a voice tells me that it doesn't exist; perhaps I should check it before I try it again, I'm advised. I'm over my blond head in this search. I need
Kathleen, and she's not answering her phone.

Something's wrong. Her silence. We started out so well,
clues, tea, touches. And now, a week later, she's missing.
And I haven't done anything to find out why, like a friend
would, concerned only with the new woman I'm trying to
become.. I need to work on the self-centered old woman I

still am. I put the latest clue aside, escape into a Sue Grafton novel, let someone else besides me solve mysteries for a day.

11

When I wake up the next morning, I turn over expecting to see Art's back. How long will I keep doing this? Forgetting that he is dead and buried. My mind wanders to that night at Jake's, the waitress, the dinner receipt, the cheerful connection with Kathleen. But we didn't talk about Brian, then or later. Thoughtless. Selfish. A person has to give as well as receive in a friendship, and that's what's becoming a surprising possibility between the two of us if I don't mess it up by not doing my part.

I find my slippers and dial Kathleen and Brian's number, but only the message machine answers. "Just wanted to say thank you again for Jake's, and for the walks," I say into the receiver and hang up. Coffee. Then I'll try again. I am pushing Mr. Coffee's ON button when the phone rings. I hope it's Kathleen, but a male voice responds to my greeting.

"Mrs. Finlay? This is Sergeant Durrell."

For a moment I'm confused. I'd put this man away somewhere in the back pockets of my obsession, not willing to untangle Art's death, only what he'd been up to before he died. I take a deep breath. "Yes?"

"We're about to close Arthur Finlay's file, and we have only one question that relates to the cause of death. We did not find any evidence of psychotropic drugs or sedatives in the containers you provided, so the guess is that he got them from someone other than his doctor."

I exhale, manage an "Okay."

"The coroner has determined that the drugs he found were not sufficient to cause death, even with his alcohol reading, either by accident or by his own hand."

Apparently not suicide. "I see." But there's more.

"He wonders, however, about the beta blocker, atenolol, Mr. Finlay was supposedly taking, prescribed by his doctor. His blood work did not indicate the presence of that drug. The prescription has to be confirmed by the doctor at regular intervals, which Dr. Blakely said he did a couple of months ago. However, the pharmacy where the prescription was sent has no record of your husband ever picking up the last order. In fact, the pills are still waiting on the pick-up shelf."

I tuck the phone under my chin and pour myself a cup of coffee. What has this to do with me? I don't know what a beta blocker is. The name atenolol is only vaguely familiar. "And is this important, now that he's gone? My husband was closemouthed about his medications. I know very little about what he was taking. How could this affect the decision about cause of death?"

The line is silent and then detective clears his throat, as if he's just taken as bite of sandwich, his lunch, I'm guessing. I glance at my watch, hoping Kathleen's not trying to reach me.

"I'll let you know if anything new shows up."

When I cradle the phone, I see I have no messages. So I can't tell an absent Kathleen about the new mystery the policeman has presented.

12

It's Monday. I check the time. If Kathleen started at 6:30, she'd be walking by the next block before 7:00, and it is 7:05. She apparently isn't walking again today. I head out by myself, just as I did last week. Walking alone is okay, but not as okay as walking and talking, the blocks slipping by unnoticed. Soon I stop being disappointed at Kathleen's abandonment and become worried about it and turn back.

Brian, when he finally answers my messages on his business phone, says that Kathleen has been very involved in the children's school play. She will be freed up by the end of the week, he is sure. "Is there a problem?" he asks. I can hear papers rustling on the desk in front of him.

"Only you," I want to answer, "you and your damn smell. What's with you?" but I just say that Kathleen and I have a project that I am looking forward to getting back to when Kathleen has time. "I'm enjoying her company," I add, and the line is silent for a beat or two until Brian says, "Good" and hangs up.

Something is wrong. I'll go it alone, this search for Art, without my partner, just as I did on this morning's walk. Whatever is happening with Kathleen is as important to her as the contents of the WHY? envelope are to me. Perhaps, in this past week our friendship has foundered on a lack of trust like we've talked about. Not my own usual distrustfulness, but Kathleen's this time. No matter the cause, I would give anything for a knock at the door, her "Mom" at this moment.

I slip my hand into the manila envelope. I pull out the dollar bill with the telephone number on it and reach for the phone.

My fingers twitch as I dial and listen for someone to answer. The phone rings four times, then a bell tinkles, and I hear, "This call is being transferred..." A second voice, melodic and self-assured, says, "Washington, CDC social worker. I'm not here right now. Please leave a message, and I'll get back to you."

I can't come up with anything to say and hang up. A female voice, mature but younger than I, beautiful, hair lying silkily on her shoulders, skinny, dressed in flowing silk, manicured nails and slinky stiletto sandals. Perhaps the sight of my own vein-crossed hands clutching the receiver has brought on this image, and the fact that I haven't shaved my legs in months, let alone dealt with the fungus in the toenail poking out from my slipper. I sit down, tuck my hairy legs under the table, lean on my elbows to steady my nerves, breathe deeply once, twice, and I dial again. I ask the lovely electronic voice if she knows Art Finlay, and if so, I, a friend of his, have an important message for her. I add my phone number and hang up.

Maybe I shouldn't have given my number. Maybe this woman already knows the number and will know I'm a wife, not a friend. But Art never received calls at home. I glance out the kitchen window and spot a spark of green popping out of one the pots on the terrace. The hellebore is doing its winter thing and probably needs some encouragement. I push aside the screen door, set the phone on the step, and try to remember where I put the fish oil. I am finished feeding the hellebore and the crocuses that are also stirring optimistically in the warming air when the phone rings.

The woman's voice is not as calm as it had been on the message. "This is Ginnie Washington. You have a message for me? From Art? Where is he?"

"Art is dead."

"Dead? What do you mean?"

I inhale, then let the words come. "Ginnie, is it? This is Edith, Art's wife. He died weeks ago, heart attack, it seems.

This number was written on a dollar bill I found in his pocket. I was curious..."

"I saw him a month or so ago. He was fine."

What sounds like either a gasp or a sob wobbles over the line. "God, I'm shocked. His wife? He never mentioned you. I thought he was a widower or something. Grown son, right?" Ginnie stops talking, maybe waiting for an answer.

I mostly hear the "never mentioned" part and let that sink in before I say, "I need to get a few answers to questions that Art's death have brought up. For instance, why did Art need a social worker? You are just one mystery of several he's left dangling. I apparently didn't know my husband very well. I need your help."

"Like?"

"Would you meet me for coffee today or tomorrow? Somewhere convenient for you? It won't take long."

"I'll be out of town until next week but I want to talk to you when I'm back. Maybe Monday afternoon?" Ginnie seems to be flipping her appointment book, then she adds, "I just can't remember giving him my number, just my card. And I don't have his number either. Perhaps Latisha wrote it down."

A silent beat. "You're right. We should talk. Monday at ten, at Cuppa's. Do you know it?"

I have noticed Cuppa's ads in the Oregonian. "Yes, in the Oyster district, right? Ten is good. I'll be wearing a red jacket. And you?"

"I'll be taking a break from work. Probably my purple suit. See you in the morning." Ginnie, wearer of purple, is gone. On high heels, I bet. Latisha.

I'm dying to tell Kathleen about Ginnie. And Latisha. I dial. No answer. Another mystery, and I'm pretty sure it doesn't involve immersion in Winston and Meg's school activities. I hadn't walked this morning, really, only a few blocks. I could walk up Fremont Street, over to Shaver, and by Evergreen Grade School, casually, as if I were just meandering by, not expecting to run into Kathleen, of course. But if I did, perhaps I could ask my daughter-in-law what in the hell is going on. No, not like that. "I've missed you," I'll say. "I have a purple suit to tell you about."

I put on my shoes, my wool jacket, push my red knit cap in my pocket, and head out. When I get to the school, its parking lot is empty except for one car, probably the custodian's, the windows dark, the playground enlivened by three kids in puffy down jackets climbing on the play structure. Their mother probably doesn't trust warm January days, I think, as I step up and try the door.

"Teacher training day," a child's voice informs me. "No school!"

Rain drops splatter on the sidewalk, and I pull out my cap. One thing you can trust in this town is that it will rain in January, warm or not. I hope the three kids' jackets are waterproof. Down takes forever to dry. I know about wet down jackets. I think of my old friend Lynne and realize I need to phone her.

13

I had been so excited about the trip. Twenty years ago.
Lynne had finally divorced Tim when she could no longer
take his massive bi-polar bouts resulting from his refusal to
take his meds. In a celebration of the first divorce in our
coffee klatch, she invited me and Eleanor to join her at a
mountain lodge for a weekend of cross-country skiing. Of the
three of us, only Eleanor had actually skied before, but the
lodge was offering lessons. Off with the old and on with the
new, the invitation read and even at forty-five that slogan
was meaningful to all three of us, now that our children no
longer needed tending. However, Eleanor's daughter was
scheduled to have her baby that week, a new kind of tending, and so only Lynne and I went, I wearing borrowed

clothes from Eleanor, including her ski pants and a down jacket.

Art had sent me off with, "Don't expect me to take care of you when you come home with a broken leg." And probably a ha.

In the late morning after we'd driven to the lodge, we got the maps and skis, and headed out, following the finger of the tanned young woman from the ski shop who got us organized and sent us toward White Horse Gulch. "A great place to begin," she called after us.

"I thought all we had to do was relax and glide," I complained, my thighs burning, after a few hours of trudging uphill through snow, my poles bracing a crumbling stance. Lynne moaned and flopped sideways against a snow hump. We agreed it was time to go back to the lodge and have a glass of wine and maybe some French fries. We had earned a reward or two, we told each other.

"Then we can go out and try again," Lynne added. Two glasses of wine later, we decided to wait to ski until the next day. "Shouldn't do too much all at once," Lynne said, signaling the waiter. We ordered a couple of hamburgers. Along with the burgers came two men in fuzzy after-ski boots and wind-burned faces.

"Care if we join you?

Lynne beamed. "Of course not."

I felt a little leery, having taught my child to never talk to strangers, but the grin on Lynne's face made me shut my mouth, and the men pulled out chairs and ordered another round of drinks as they introduced themselves. They were fiftyish, good-looking in a men-on-a-break kind of way, tanned, oiled, good teeth. They laughed and talked about themselves, and we listened and wondered where this would lead. At least, I did. Lynne seemed not to care as the good-humored man sitting next to her patted her arm.

"You've probably haven't seen the suites here at the lodge, have you?" he asked, after learning our room featured bunk beds and a bathroom down the hall. "Come on. I'll show you ours. It's great." Lynne nodded, and with that, he led my wide-eyed friend away.

"Another drink?" Ron, the man left at my side, signaled to the waiter although I had waved no more over my glass. Sipping at my refilled glass, I listened as Ron talked about his divorce, his kids who were angry at him, his loneliness. "I wasn't meant to live alone," he said. He was quiet for a moment, his hand wiping across his eyes. "Hell, I shouldn't be talking to you like this." He reached out for my wrist, touched it. "But you are a very good listener. Thank you."

I realized I liked him, too.

He drained his mug and shoved back his chair. "I want to repay you. Let's go out on my snowmobile and take a ride on the mountain."

He wasn't inviting me to his bedroom. "Okay, why not?" I answered, maybe a little disappointed.

Outside, bundled up in down jackets, we found his snowmobile lined up with others along the road. With a roar, we rolled away and crunched down a trail away from the lodge and into the woods. Ron waved at others moving on the same sort of machines as they passed. Red-cheeked and laughing, everyone seemed to be having a good time, and I laughed too, not releasing my hold on Ron's waist. At first the cool breeze was exhilarating, and I was glad for my down jacket. An hour later the sky blackened, and the jacket got too warm. I wished I could let go of Ron to unzip it. "Getting muggy," I yelled into his ear.

He shouted back over his shoulder, "Going to rain." He stopped and I let go of him. "Looks like we got a temperature change. We should go back."

I glanced ahead down the trail and saw that no one was in front of us or following us. The lodge had disappeared somewhere behind a high ridge. I grabbed Ron's jacket as the snowmobile lurched into the softer snow and eased back onto the trail. We headed the way we had come, and I was disappointed.

Then the motor sputtered, and the snowmobile stopped growling. Ron got out, jiggled something, poked at the unmoving track. "Fuck. We're out of gas." His words were punctuated by a large splat of wet snow landing on his forehead. Both of us looked up, and I saw that what had been a lovely soft white blanket lying on the limbs of the evergreens along the trail was breaking apart, sloughing off, dropping to the ground all around us.

"We're low on the mountain. The warm air hits here first, and—" He scanned the black sky. "—will probably bring some rain. Let's start walking. Someone will come by and pick us up." He took my arm and supported me until my legs got used to earth again.

Ron's after-ski boots slipped and skidded in the melting snow with each step. My cross-country boots, too big, and my socks, heavy cotton, not wool, as I had been advised, squished juicily. Not talking, except for the occasional "You okay?" we sloshed along the trail. Huge drops of rain began beating on my hood. Minutes later, I was drenched to the skin.

"I'm really cold," I whimpered.

Ron took my hand and pulled me toward a low cave under the limbs of a small pine, and we crawled into it. The cold ground was still frozen, and soon I was shivering so hard I couldn't talk. When I closed my eyes, I had a fleeting vision of a little girl who died curled up in the snow. I could almost feel the stiff pages of my grandma's old book, a sad tale meant to make kids cry. In the drawing, the dead little girl had looked quite peaceful. Perhaps I will be, too, I thought. Anything would be better than the shuddering my body was doing right then.

"Here. Take my coat." Ron pulled his arms out of his wet jacket and laid it across my back. "I got you into this. I need to leave you here, go find help."

"Absolutely not!" My words stuttered out between frozen lips. "Not alone! We can share our coats and sweaters." Another scene from different survival story surfaced. "Warm bodies. I read about this." I began to unzip my soaked jacket, and he asked, "Are you sure?" At my screech of a yes, he took off his wool shirt, I pulled my sweater over my head, and when we had bared our chests, we wrapped our discarded clothes over us. I clung to him, pressing myself against him, tepid skin against tepid skin, the both of us swaddled in wet garments.

We didn't move and didn't talk as darkness settled in. The evening air cooled, and our chests offered little warmth. I was almost dozing, imagining Art's ha when he heard the news of my freezing to death on a mountain. Suddenly headlights pierced through the tree boughs, and we heard familiar voices call our names. We stumbled out, dragging pieces of clothing behind us, and we were greeted by Lynne and the suite-guy. "We found you!" Lynn exclaimed; then she noticed our near-naked bodies, and she threw her coat and her arms around me.

A small note in the Oregonian a few days later spoke of the unusual warming of the lower altitudes of the mountain and mentioned several climbers who had been forced back down the mountain once they saw the rain coming, the possibility of slides imminent, and a couple on a snowmobile who had been rescued by friends after a malfunction of their machine. After Art read the article, touched the down jacket dripping into the bathtub as I lay in bed wracked with coughs and wheezes, and heard snatches of Lynne's and my whispered phone calls, he put two and two together. He demanded to know who the man was.

"I don't really know. Just someone we met and who invited me to go on his snowmobile. I don't even know his last name."

Art ha-ed. "I knew it was a mistake to let you go off like that, with a woman whose marriage was probably destroyed by tricks like this." He kicked at the mattress, might have wanted to kick me, and snarled, "Slut."

Even in the echo of that word, I could feel the almost-warm skin of a man who cared enough about me to hold me close and safe.

Now, only in late-night memory tours do I ever feel a twinge of guilt. Mostly only joy, actually.

14

This morning, the person who looks out at me when I brush my teeth is vaguely familiar. My hair is still curly, not sleek as Marie's blow dryer made it, and it stands out an inch or so from the top of my head. But it is yellow, not white. I examine my face. I've always disliked old faces and young hair. And now I have them both. I pull back on the skin just under my ears, and the deep lines from the corners of my mouth to my jaw disappear; well, not quite, but the erosion that has taken place, beginning at the nostrils, lessens. A number of valleys, creek beds, head south from my lips toward my chin, a weather-worn landscape. Beautiful in the wild, not so good on an old lady. Older woman. Even my vocabulary needs adjustment.

It's time to call Lynne, make amends for my silence of the past weeks. And maybe have a little lunch, find out what she is doing, worrying about, glad about. Get back to that trust that once bloomed between coffee sips and wine glass clinks, sick husbands, bruised wrists, maybe not yet lost in the flurry of getting older, waving goodbye to children and children's children on Christmas morning, letting go of life instead of grasping at it.

And if anyone knows facial landscapes, Lynne will.

"I'm thinking of having a little work done," I tell her after a moment of joyful connection. "Not Barbara Walters, maybe just a tune-up. I need to move forward like you've always done, not backward like my face does."

Lynne snickers, says, "Just a minute, Honey, this is important." Back at the phone she explains, "He's my Wednesday/Saturday guy. He sometimes takes a while to leave."

"And you have a Tuesday/Sunday guy?"

"God, no." Lynn lowers her voice. "I need time for myself, too, you know. So how are you?"

We haven't talked since the week Art died and then only a hug and a "We'll talk." Which we haven't until now. "I'm doing okay, working to settle things after Art's…"

"The lawyer things are awful, aren't they?"

"No, all that's going okay. In fact, I'm hoping to let loose of Art entirely very soon. Besides just wanting to hear how you are, which makes me quite envious." I need to change the subject, to go slower, to not talk about Art yet, move into Lynne's zone. "I'm also wondering who your plastic surgeon is. If that's not too presumptuous. I did notice your neck at Art's celebration of life."

"We've got to get together with Eleanor! She has no upper arm flab, and her boobs, damn, well, her husband likes big boobs. I don't, personally, but no accounting for tastes, and she gave me Dr. Johansen's name when I got worried about my neck. I'm also considering my earlobes. Are yours hanging down to your shoulders like mine?" She pauses to take a breath. "No, of course they aren't. You don't wear earrings. You should."

"Dr. Johansen?"

"Peter Johansen. The best." Her words are muffled. "Okay, honey. I'm through talking." Lynne comes back, whispers, "He likes a little Wednesday nooner. Sometimes I do too. I'll call you."

It is obvious to me that today Lynne is not into the kind of intimacy I'm seeking, the kind in which one can confess to maybe killing a husband.

I go back to the bathroom mirror, stretch back a half-inch of skin on each side of my ears, let it snap back. Back-lit, I notice my cracks don't look that bad.

I'll try Kathleen again. At the third ring, my daughter-in-law answers. Instead of explaining her absence, Kathleen says, "I'm glad you called, Edith. I need a little help, only a few nights. I know you are busy, but..."

I am so pleased with the request I don't even ask what it is. "Of course. Right now?" I hesitate because I'd like to tell her about a woman in a purple suit, but no matter. "I can come."

"This weekend. I want the kids to feel okay and happy, and they will with you. I can't explain right now, but Brian and I will be going somewhere, we haven't decided where, and we will be talking. I wish I could tell you more, but I promised him I would not say anything now or maybe ever."

Her wavering voice sounds familiar. Like my own, the day I confessed to my mother that I was pregnant. Pleading for something. Love, probably, on my part. Perhaps Kathleen is asking for something similar.

"Can you take the kids for a couple of days?"

"Of course. I've been meaning to teach them one of the fundamental skills in life and this will be a good time."

"Skills?"

"How to make the world's best mac and cheese. I've got all of the essential ingredients and a little ham if we want to dress it up." I used to make mac and cheese with Brian. I can do it again with his children. In fact, I need to, since their mother doesn't do carbs in her own kitchen.

"I'll bring them by tomorrow, after school with their sleeping bags." Kathleen hangs up without saying goodbye.

15

Kathleen arrives with the children on Friday afternoon. She also brings sliced carrots, apples, unsalted nuts, yogurt, and for dessert, she explains, a whole-wheat muffin, no butter please. Dinner will be the promised mac and cheese with a side dish of steamed spinach which blooms greenly from the bag she carries in her arms. Kathleen looks exhausted despite the smile she's planted on her lips. Her hair apparently has been overlooked in the rush to gather food. Straggles trail out of the center of the bun and curl on her collar, and she pokes a finger at them. "Sunday morning," she promises, as she stops at the door. "Scrambled eggs would be good.

You have eggs? And by the way, I love your new hair, Mom."

The Mom again. My daughter-in-law isn't just worried about eggs. "Yep, we've got everything. Have a good time." I suspect that a good time isn't the purpose of this unusual depositing of kids, and that Brian and Kathleen aren't going away from home.

Friday evening we lay out the sleeping bags, sample a new cookie dough ice cream, and they read themselves to sleep with the books in their backpacks.

The next morning, "Cartoons," the kids suggest when I ask what they want to do.

"Does your mother let you watch TV?"

Meg looks at Winston. "Sometimes. For an hour or so. When we've done our chores."

"I'm assuming you've both done your chores sometime this week." I turn on the television, and after a few minutes, I understand that today's cartoons are not the cartoons of forty years ago. These are sermons, a Sunday School in color, vegetables teaching children how to treat each other, why being good is better than being bad, and in one short segment, not to bully your sister because in the long run, she'll make you pay. What happened, I wonder, to the Road Runner and Coyote, who were in trouble all of the time, no learning experience to be had? And Bugs Bunny? But once I get used to the fast pace of the dialogue, I am pulled into

the stories and am disappointed when SpongeBob slips behind a wall of advertisements.

"I'm bored." Winston is flailing in the corner of the sofa
as if he's in pain. "What else is there to do?" For the moment, Meg ignores her brother, eyes focused on a Kellogg
tiger.

"And Grandma, why is your hair yellow?" Meg has also
become bored enough to notice my new hair during the next
ad. "And your cheeks so red?"

"I'm practicing to become a new me," I answer. "I believe change is good thing for people. Maybe next time my
hair will be ginger."

"Ginger?" Winston is squinting at me, imagining.

"Orange."

"I'd like to change me," Meg says. "I'd like blue hair and
pink lips."

"Green, curly hair," Winston adds. "For me. And tattoos
up my arms."

Why not? "Come on, guys. Your wishes are about to
come true." Food dye? It'll wash out, like it does from one's
fingers after dyeing eggs. It should, at least. Tattoos will be
easy. What else? My grandchildren giggle and follow me into
the kitchen, watch me reach for the bottles, bring out the
stool and chair that will allow them to stand at the sink and
become new people, hair-wise.

I hope the blue and green will also wash out from my
towels. At least I have thought ahead that far. I don't even

try to imagine getting it out of the stringy hair that drips onto toweled shoulders. And I am disappointed when my old foam curlers won't stay rolled, and Winston and I have to admit defeat on the curly wish.

I feel a little crazy, in a good way. As if I am a kid myself, looking for trouble, wondering how far I can go without getting myself in trouble. I hear myself say, "Did I hear tattoos? Stay where you are, and I'll get the tattoo gun." Markers, bought and forgotten in a drawer at Christmas. I check the box. Washable. Thank God. "What'll it be?"

The boy is first. I suggest a triceratops, and he tells me that at ten he is way too old for dinosaurs. He settles for a space rocket zooming off one arm. And Meg?

Meg isn't sure about tattoos. "Maybe a butterfly on my ankle." That accomplished, she adds, "I want pink lips and red cheeks like yours and Mama's."

"And maybe a mustache for your brother?"

We head for the makeup drawer in the bathroom, a drawer until just recently rarely opened. A few minutes later the children take a peek at themselves in the mirror. Meg says, "I'm a different person."

Winston frowns. "Not really, you still act like yourself."

"So who should she act like?"

"A famous movie star. Maybe Julia Roberts."

"And who will you act like?"

Winston takes another look at himself. "Matthew Broderick with green hair. And a mustache."

I don't know who Matthew Broderick is. Not a mass
murderer, I'm pretty sure. Or even a zombie, which I believe
is becoming a craze. Kathleen wouldn't allow people like
that into her children's lives, even in the movies. "Okay.
And I don't think we are really new people unless other people think so, too. Where shall we go?" A walk through the
park or visiting one of my neighbors would do it.

"McDonald's." Both children grin at me.

Oh, why not? I've been saying "Why not?" a lot this
morning. It seems like a good way to look at things, things
being what they are. "Well, new people probably should go
to new places. I've never been there, and I bet you haven't
either."

"Once, when Daddy was in charge of us, and he burned
the beans."

We walk to McDonald's, on the way watching people's
reactions when they see green and blue hair, tattoos, pink
lips. And a grinning, spiky-haired grandma. Somewhere during the next hour I realize I haven't had so much fun since I
can't remember when. My red cheeks ache from smiling.

On the way back, we walk to the park, our new selves
slightly smudged but still attention-getting, and then we
make the mac and cheese, Meg and Winston standing on a
stool or kneeling on a chair to reach the counter as they stir
and grate. I did this almost forty years ago. Brian was about
eight, wanted to learn to cook, despite his father's ha, and
the two of us did just as I and my grandchildren are doing

now. A crazy, crazy thought interrupts my stirring. If history does repeat itself, is it possible that Brian is reenacting his father's story of infidelity? Brian, the bright, sensitive son who loved mac and cheese? I have to turn my head away from the bubbling pots and the blue and green heads and wipe my eyes on a paper towel. What does any of this mean? Anything, at all?

"Grandma, the mac is boiling over!" As I turn down the burner and uncover the pot, I have an answer of sorts. One lives for the moments like this one.

I decide that before they go to bed, the children should take a shower to remove the day-old evidence, but not before I take several pictures that will remind me of this lovely day. For the albums. The blue and the green, with several applications of shampoo, wash out, and the tattoos disappear under the natural sponge.

I've found a couple of the old children's books I've stored for years, and they quiet the kids down. Make Way for Ducklings, Ten Thousand Cats, Lyle the Crocodile. For younger children and for sensitive older ones who want to please their grandmother. "Old stories," I say. "Almost as old as me." I nap a bit as the children page through their father's worn picture books.

They are back to themselves, and perhaps I am also, whatever that means. For right now, it means lying on the floor between two damp-haired children in sleeping bags, holding a book on my chest, and reading about a girl who shouldn't have taken a bite of that apple.

"Boring," declares Winston, and he turns his back away from the light and falls asleep.

"Keep going, Grandma," Megan commands.

In the morning, at the sound of the doorbell, I hide the cut-up veggies and yogurt at the back of the fridge, stuff the wilting spinach in the garbage and then go to let Kathleen in. My daughter-in-law's eyes swim in gray pools. The hair hasn't improved.

"Thank you so much, Edith," she says as she shuffles the backpacks and her children toward the car. "I'll call you. Soon.   "

16

What does one wear to a meeting with a satin-voice in a purple suit and heels? On Monday morning, I answer my question and get ready to meet her. Jeans, the pair without the hole in the knee caused by an ungraceful stumble over a planter box a while back, and a top that settles over the jeans in a somewhat narrow facsimile of a profile. My red jacket, and if it is raining, my red knit cap. If I relax my lips a little, the crevasses at the edges of my lips turn into pleasant, non-threatening valleys. How long can one maintain pleasant valleys, I wonder as I head out to Cuppa to receive what might be really unpleasant information.

I sit at the table, my untasted latte in front of me, and wait. A woman walks through the door, glances around, finds my red jacket, and points a finger at me. "I'll get my coffee and be right there," she calls as she heads toward the barista.

I had been right about the middle-age, the great suit, the heels, but dead wrong on everything else. This woman has a wide, white-toothed smile, hands that move like dancers when she speaks, and black hair gathered into bun at the back of her head, a white orchid perching on it. Her bracelet is jade, the color of her cheerful shoes. Lynne has a word for a woman who looks like this: fabulous. And I'm glad the distracting orchid and the shoes aren't visible when she sits down in front of me. But her green eyes, her smooth, light-brown face are.

"Hello!" She holds out a hand, and I take it, feel the firm skin, the warm welcome it contains.

I hesitate. "How do you know Art?" I bring my cooled cup to my lips.

"I'm a social worker, a department head at Children's Services, have been for years. I've met lots of parents and lots of kids, but Art and Latisha were something else, as you may know."

The coffee is bitter. I set the cup down. "I know nothing. Tell me."

"Art is dead." Not a question, and continues, not waiting for my response. "Normally, I'd feel uncomfortable talking about a client, but Art wasn't a client, more of a friend who needed a little help from someone like me who knows the complicated social services system. But with him gone, well, a lot is now explained. Latisha has felt abandoned these past weeks. Now she'll know why. Won't make her feel any better, of course, but she won't continue to imagine he's left her on purpose."

The woman is speaking in some sort of foreign language. Abandoned? Left her? Who is this person Art has managed to make feel bad? "Start at the beginning. I don't understand a word you're saying."

Ginnie pauses, pushes aside her cup. She seems to be making a decision. "I met Art last fall when he came into my office looking for a child. She had been given up for adoption eighteen years earlier, and he wanted to make contact, find out how her life had gone, if she wanted to meet her father. He gave me the name of her birth mother, the girl's date of birth. I actually knew the girl because she had entered a foster home when she was fourteen, after her adoptive father went to prison and her adoptive mother died. I explained to him that because she's eighteen, she could begin her own search for her birth parents. Perhaps we should let her decide if she wants to do this. She was about to enter college. I said perhaps the timing was wrong."

"I still don't get it. What reason did Art give you for wanting to find this girl, this Latisha?"

"I spoke inappropriately when I gave you her name. A mistake." Ginnie Washington looks away, touches an earring. "I regret it." Then she seems to forgive herself and continues. "At first, he didn't give a reason. I assumed he was her birth father..."

"Art and I were married eighteen years ago and long before that. I would have known, wouldn't I, if he had taken up with another woman, had a child?"

No, I probably wouldn't have. Eighteen years ago my only son was about to marry a woman I didn't like, and I was obsessed, a crazy person, in fact, as I lay awake nights and plotted to break them up. Even at this moment I'm embarrassed to remember that I hired a private detective to try to catch Kathleen in some indiscriminate act.

After the detective reported that she'd had a date with a male in a small restaurant during which she had broken into tears and left the table, I invited her to coffee in my kitchen and accused her of being a two-timer.

I could barely hear her quiet, furious response. "I can't believe you! He's an old friend from high school, a sick friend who told me that night that he had leukemia. Yes, I cried." She stood, reached out, took a step toward me, and for a moment, I thought she might hit me. Instead, she grabbed her purse, slammed the door, and walked away. And when he heard about our meeting, my accusations, Brian walked away from me, too. It took me days to find the courage to apologize, and more time for the apology to be accepted by both him and Kathleen. And to get invited to the wedding. They were that angry. I blamed menopause, but I began to understand that my meanness grew from my envy of their happiness.

Ginnie doesn't answer my question. "Art gave me a phone number and told me that he'd like to talk to her if she wanted to know more about her roots. I did a background check on him, and a wife appeared in his records, but he never spoke of her. I supposed she wasn't in the picture anymore. He claimed that an interested party asked him to find out how she was doing. Like I said, I assumed that he was the interested party but wasn't ready to reveal that fact. When I asked Latisha, she smiled and said she'd like to talk to him, too.

She must have seen my eyebrows rise in disbelief. "I know," she adds. "But Latisha is eighteen. She's on her own now. She has the right to make her own decisions about Art. And she did. She had dinner with him a number of times after I introduced them, and I went along a time or two. He was very interested in her plans for her future, her education, what she wanted to do with her life. She told me when I called to see how she was doing that he'd given her money for her books at school when she mentioned needing to get a loan from a friend. 'Not a loan, this,' he told her, handing her an envelope. 'A prize for being a good kid.'"

"Does Latisha have black hair done up in corkscrews, big hair falling to her shoulders. And is she black?"

"Yes. Light-skinned like me."

I haven't given much thought to Ginnie's skin color; the green eyes spoke first, diverting most other impressions except how stunning the woman was. Maybe that's why the waitress at Jake's hadn't noticed either. Jake's. "Did Art ever get really angry when you were out with him?"

She shrugged. "Once, maybe, when he tried to buy a celebratory drink for Latisha. He was usually very quiet and intense whenever I saw him. Like he had something on his mind."

"Depressed?"

"No, more like determined. Why?"

"Because I'm beginning to believe that he may have misused his drugs, intentionally killed himself."

"Oh, no." Ginnie shakes her head. "Doesn't seem right. He seemed very pleased to have found Latisha finally."

And that doesn't sound right, Art pleased. A gray veil of guilt settles over me, and I close my eyes against it. When had it begun, my coldness? Eighteen years ago? Is it possible that I could have sensed his infidelity? Like Kathleen, smelled another woman on him without knowing what that scent meant? Had I pulled away even more then, never to return? Or, the other possibility, this winter, on one of his night-walks, had he met a charming young woman who listened to him, who made him feel like a man again, who needed him in ways he hadn't been needed in years, and he had figured out a way to make her part of his life?

Daughter? Lover? Both shocking scenarios force my eyes to open, me to say, "I'd like to meet Latisha."

17

I go home, take a sleeping pill, wrap myself in my quilt, and wait for soothing darkness. A frenzy of scenes involving Art and a shadowy young woman flash across my inner screen, make me sick to my stomach. Finally, they slide away and I do, too.

When the phone rings, startles me, I almost ignore it. But it might be Kathleen. It isn't. A soft voice asks, "Is this Edith?" The voice adds, "This is Latisha?"

The question mark at the end of her sentence makes her a teenager or close to it. "Yes?" I respond, hearing my own question mark. "Ginnie's friend?"

"Ginnie's client, mostly. Art's friend."

"Art," I manage. "My husband. My dead husband."

"That's why I'm calling. I didn't know he had died. I feel so bad and..."

Is she crying? "We need to talk. About Art," I say. Art has made this girl sad. That both disgusts and intrigues me. That he and Latisha had connected in a way that makes her cry because he is dead. After forty-some years of marriage, I have hardly dropped a tear, maybe only once or twice but not about him—only about a song he used to sing. The tears I shed are about not knowing him. This girl's are about knowing him.

"I'd like that," she says. "Where is good for you?"

We decide on a new Taiwanese teashop located about in the middle of our East-West neighborhoods. "They have bubble tea," Latisha says.

"I don't know bubble tea, but I'm open to it," I answer, and I think as I hang up, God, make me open to Latisha and bubble tea, and not want to kill her.

I look at the list of bubble teas Scotch-taped to the wall and just about give up. Do people actually drink rosewater? With green tea and tapioca? At $3.95 a glass?

"I like the mocha with everything," a voice suggests behind me. I step back and look directly in a mass of black ringlets hanging like curtains on each side of smiling white teeth. I have to search a second for the eyes hiding behind curls, and when I find them, they are smiling, too. "If you like coffee...I'm Latisha," the girl says holding out her hand.

Latisha is a big girl. Her big hair is just right for her six-foot frame. I am amazed both at the size of her body and the hair, but mostly at the strong clasp of the fingers that hold mine.

"I'm Edith," I say. "Order for me and for you. I haven't a clue." I work on sounding friendly.

We wait at the counter, watching the server mix our drinks. I can see that it would be easy to poison someone from behind this counter: the jammy paste, the liquids, the colorful spoonfuls of unknown substances that might be lethal. Even the cupful of round, transparent pellets sinking to the bottom of our glasses.

"Tapioca, big time," Latisha says, apparently sensing my discomfort.

I hand the server a ten-dollar bill and take my drink to a table by the window. When Latisha joins me, our heads bend into the huge straws, and I risk a sip. Sweet, a coffee flavor. A pea-sized bubble flows into my mouth and down my throat. "Are you supposed to chew?" I ask when I understand I'm not going to choke. She seems warm, cheerful, not my idea of a mistress. Of course, what do I know about mistresses?

"Some do. Some don't." Latisha laughs, chews. Then she goes serious. A hand whips the curls back from her face, and strands rest awhile behind her ears. "How did Art die?"

"In bed. Without warning. On Christmas Day." I wait as the girl blinks, takes a sip from the straw, lifts her head. "How did you know Art?" I ask.

"Ginnie gave me his phone number, and I called him. He said a friend of his had been looking for me and that friend cared about me, but he couldn't meet me right then. Art said his friend would help me out since I was getting too old to be taken care of by Children's Services. And Art would be the..."

"Go-between?" When had Art ever done any so-called friend that kind of favor? "So did you ever meet this friend?"

"No, but Art said that the friend would pay my fees so that I could start college this spring. And he would pay room and board to my foster parents so they could keep me for a while." Latisha smiled. "That was the best thing of all. I didn't know where I would live." The drink burbles, and she sucks up the last of the bubbles clustered at the bottom of the glass. She looks up. "That's about it, I guess."

No, it's not. "Did you have ribs at Boo's Soul very often?"

Latisha nods. "My favorite place. He said he liked it, too, but not the ribs so much. Art never did come to this here place, though. He said the idea of bubbles scared him."

At least my husband and I had one thing is common. A fear of bubble tea. My own bubbles lie waiting at the bottom of drink. I gather them in my mouth, feel their soft, firm presence and chew. Just like tapioca pudding, only bigger and without the pudding. Fish eyes, my cousin used to tease me. Really big fish eyes. For the first time this afternoon, I am relaxing in this girl's warm gaze. Then I remember why I'm here. "He gave you money?"

"Sometimes. Spending money, he said."

"And you met him how often?"

"Once or twice with Ginnie, and then once a week or so since last fall at Boo's Soul or at other places." Latisha looks down at her hands, pulls her shoulder bag into her lap. "I didn't know about you." She takes a Kleenex out of her bag, blows a little, mostly dabbing quietly at her eyes. "I'm sorry if that was wrong."

The Kleenex is pink.

"So Art didn't mention he was married, had a son and grandchildren?"

"He mentioned the son, talked about having a couple of little kids around sometimes, said you all were big on Christmas. But mostly, he asked about how I was doing, what classes I was taking, did I need anything? He was kind of like having a nice grandpa. Sometimes he gave me advice."

"Advice? Like what?"

Latish blushed. "I had a boyfriend, sort of. I told Art about him, and Art told me that I had to take care of myself—you know, be safe."

Shit!

"He gave me the address of Planned Parenthood, but I already knew it because my foster parents told me the same thing. He never brought it up again. Which is okay because Leandro and I never did get together and nobody had to worry anymore."

I suspect that worry isn't a problem to Latisha. Worry is what parents do. At least I, a mother, used to, still do. I am not aware that Art ever worried about kids, his own especially. Until Latisha.

My bubbles are gone. Latisha is looking at her watch.

"Sorry," she says when she sees I have noticed. "I'm working part time. At a wig shop. I'm due at 4:00, and I'll be getting there on TriMet. The bus is due in five minutes."

I should drive her, I think. However, the window of opportunity has closed. Latisha has her bag on her shoulder and her firm hand out. "Can we do this again?" she asks.

"Of course," I answer, squeezing the girl's fingers, not wanting to lose this contact. Not until I have earned the truth, at least. Lover? The suggestion about Planned Parenthood may have come for a much different reason. Daughter? His belated interest in her studies, life. I'll never know unless we meet again. Maybe not bubble tea. "How do you feel about Starbucks?"

"Or Cuppa? Bus nearby. When?"

"A week from today?"

Latisha pulls out her planner, scribbles. "Got it. See you," she calls.

I go home and return to the quilt and the pill and the frantic impossible visions.

18

Twice in the past two days, people have said, "See you soon," and I have come to not trust that promise. See you soon means "unless something more important shows up."

Well, I can do that, too. I have things I have to do, and people to see. Or bits of paper to look over one more time, allow them to lead me somewhere that makes more sense.

All I know is that Art was meeting a social worker and a young girl with really big hair, and was in fact giving her money. The social worker suspects he's the girl's what? Father? Guilt-stricken years later. And I am beginning to believe he could have been her lover. Besotted. My sick midnight thoughts come up with the idea that somehow Art had gotten Latisha's birth information, had used it to make contact through the social worker with her.

At least the pink Kleenex has an explanation. Art had picked it up, unusually neat, tucked it into his pocket. Forgot it.

I am about to open the Why envelope in an effort to quell the churning that is rattling my waking hours when I hear a knock, unlock my door, open it and am greeted by a frenzy of yips, paws clawing at me, and two children yelling. I let them in and collapse against the sofa.

"What?"

"A surprise, Grandma." Meg speaks up, grinning as if she's about to burst into bubble tea. "We decided you need a friend. Here's Brody."

I feel a warm tongue slathering my leg. "Brody?"

"A really good, gentle, older dog just right for you," Winston chimes in, standing very straight behind his giggling sister. "Brody is a part golden, part something else, and he has the best brown eyes of any dog we looked at." My grandson gives me an unflinching stare with his own brown eyes, daring me to say no.

I don't know what to feel. Anger? A little. Dismay, definitely. Interest in the tongue making its way up my leg? Yes, in a weird sort of way. "I don't want a dog," I say, the way I used to say, "Clean your room." Not convincing, even to me.

Kathleen moves into the tangle of legs and tongue. "We talked about you being alone here, needing maybe something furry to pet. We made a trip, Edith. I drove, an accomplice—to the Humane Society, and Meg and Winston found

Brody." She glances at her children. "They feel Brody and you are meant for each other."

Brody seems to know what his role is at this moment. He sits down and smiles at me.

Before I can object, Winston adds, "We have the food, a leash, he's had his shots, and we brought a bed for him. No problem, Grandma."

It's the Grandma that gets me, warmth of that word. I feel myself caving. "You have to help, you know. I don't know about..." Brody and Meg and Winston land on me, arms and legs digging into my thighs, and I haven't felt so landed on since the clothes line full of sheets fell on me fifty years ago. Smothered. Wet. Tugged at.

We introduce Brody to the door that leads to the yard at the back of the house. Winston opens the sack and takes out several metal dishes, a box of plastic bags, and a sack of dog food. "You'll get used to it, Grandma," he assures me. The children fill his new shiny bowls with water and food.

"Where does Brody sleep?" I wonder. Dog house? Backyard?

"Dogs are pack animals. They sleep with their pack." Meg seems to be quoting a dog expert, probably the Humane Society volunteer who had okayed Brody's adoption.

"And that's me?" I'm getting the picture. "What if he snores?" A dog in my bedroom, noisy, like Art —but with rules. "He sleeps in his own bed." Boundaries are important.

"Sure, Grandma. Whatever you want. He'll do it."

Damn. That's a change. This might work out.

The children take Brody for a walk, tucking a couple of poo-bags into their jeans pockets, arguing who gets the leash first. Kathleen sinks to the sofa. "I hope you aren't angry. It was Meg's idea, to get you the dog. She says you look sad sometimes. Little kids notice things like that."

"So do old ladies. You also seem sad and tired. You've not been home when I've called. What is going on?"

Kathleen lays her head against the sofa back and closes her eyes. "We'll take Brody if he doesn't work out."

"Kathleen. Can I help?"

My daughter-in-law doesn't speak for a moment, then she raises her head and sits up, back straight, more Kathleen-like, and I'm relieved.

"Brian took ten thousand dollars from our savings account. A couple of months ago. He says he'll pay it back."

Speechless, I go to the kitchen, pour two cups of coffee, set one of them in front of Kathleen, and by then, she and I are breathing well enough for me to ask, "Why?"

"I got the bank statement, saw the withdrawal, and asked the same question. He won't tell me, except that I shouldn't worry. It's his problem, he insisted, and he's taking care of it."

Kathleen's lips barely move, her eyes fixed on her cup. "He's still going out at odd times." She looks up at me. "And I'm going out of my mind." The words crackle, break up. "I try to follow him. That's where I've been every day, wandering the streets like I'm psychotic, following him when I can find him. Most of the time he just goes to business meetings and lunches. I can't keep doing this. I've hired a private detective."

"That's not so crazy," I say, not sure if I should remind Kathleen of my own experience with a detective. I should sit next to Kathleen, maybe hold her hand. No. Kathleen's not looking for pity. Maybe a friend to listen? "You just want to find out answers. I know about that, how not knowing is worse than knowing."

I'm about to go on, but Kathleen stands up, goes to the window, pulls the drapes back. "The kids love that dog. They begged to take Brody home. I said no, not now, and they gave up too easily. They know something is wrong. I finally agreed when Meg, in tears, said you need company. When this is all over, Brody can come live with us. We may need company then, too."

I hear a burst of laughter and a sharp, happy bark. The children have found a stick, and it appears that Brody is part retriever as he skids across the grass in pursuit of it. Maybe I've always wanted a dog, without knowing it. I can imagine walking Brody, talking to him, telling him to stop snoring, even taking care of his...

"Ooo, he pooped," Meg yells. She waves at us at the window. "This is how you pick it up, Grandma." The girl pulls a plastic bag over her hand, grits her teeth, stoops to scoop up the pile. Her brother, standing back a little, says, "Way to go, Meg."

"Next time you get to do it," she answers as she runs to the garbage can and lifts the lid.

"Damn. Just like a man. Lets the woman do the cleaning up." I am not sure what tone of voice Kathleen intends. Joking? Angry?

"Cleaning up is a female gene," I answer. "Look at us, cleaning up after our husbands." We two such different women have something in common.

Winston, Meg, and Brody roar in. "He needs water," Meg shouts. The scramble for the dish, the dog's loud, eager lapping ends whatever either of us might have said next.

"We need to go, Edith. Appointments at the dentist." The dog gets hugs, then their grandma does, and then they go to the door. "I'll call you," Kathleen adds.

Another promise.

Brody's toenails tap behind me as I go to the kitchen,. "Just you and me, kid," I say as I rub his head. It's good, having someone to talk to, the churning stilled.

19

Brody hears the knock on the door first, growls in his low, protective voice, stirs on his pillow at the side of my bed. My heart beats a little faster, too, as I put down my book and pull on my robe. "Who is it?"

No answer, just another knock. Brody clicks behind me as I head to the door.

I have never before used the little peephole in the front door. I put my eye up to it and see hair, a lot of it. "Latisha?"

"Yes. Sorry to come so late. I just got off work."

I am confused. Hadn't we talked of coffee, not an unexpected drop-in on a dark night? I open the door. "Come in," I say, once I see that it is indeed the girl and that she is alone.

Latisha hesitates. "I'm not staying. I was going home after my shift, and I missed the last bus that I had to transfer to, and I couldn't find a public phone, so I walked here so maybe I could use your phone to call Helen, my foster mother?

"How did you know where I live?"

"I looked you up in the phonebook after we met. I was going to send you a thank-you note." Latisha fidgets with her jacket, as if she's about to take it off and then decides not to. "But I had a big test and I forgot."

I am not about to ask her to stay. Why would I? The very idea of her is painful, no matter what that idea is. I point to the phone on the coffee table. "Go ahead and call." I add, "Then you'll have to leave. I've got an early appointment and need to get back to sleep." Brody lies down between us, and Latisha steps over him to get to the phone.

"Hi, it's me," she says a moment later. "I missed my last bus, and I'm at a friend's house. Can you pick me up?" She listens. "Great. I'm at 72..." she looks at me for help with the address, and I give her the names of cross streets at the stop light three blocks away.

"Easier for her to find," I add. Who knows who the girl is calling and, in fact, who Latisha is. I shouldn't have opened the door in the first place. "I'll point you in the right direction, and you can start walking."

Latisha pats Brody's head. "That's cool, Mrs. Finlay." As she leaves, she turns and smiles, and I suddenly feel very bad. "I knew you'd help me. Thank you. See you next week."

I lean my head against the closed door as I turn the lock. Why am I so afraid? Of a young woman with a head of curls and teeth that shine in the porch light? A person who says thank you and tells me I'm cool. Nothing frightening about her. Is there? Only unknown. For the moment that's enough make my heart beat a little faster, my mouth go dry.

Brody has returned to his bed and is looking at me with sleep-heavy eyes. "I acted like a bitch, didn't I, dog?" An semi-alert ear twitches in agreement. I groan. "I guess you know about bitches. Well, you're going to have to deal with yet another one."

The walks I wanted to make with Kathleen I now make with Brody. For two mornings so far, we have made our ways to the dog park about a mile way, I with a pocket full of poo bags and an orange ball we found abandoned in a gutter. Even in the rain, the exercise feels good, and I have written dog raincoat on my shopping list as well as treats, whatever they are, which a fellow dog owner has told me are helpful training aids. He is probably referring to Brody's exuberant greeting, two paws pressed into his crotch, which embarrasses me but makes the man chuckle. And I'm relieved to find out that Brody only snores a little at night, and he stops when I call out his name.

When Latisha phones on Friday, I try to come up with a reason not to meet her. My days have been going quite well. I'm getting some reading done, am spending too much time talking to the dog, but he's a good listener with no problems of his own to lay on my unwilling shoulders. I also suspect that the girl needs money, now that Art is not around. But the mystery of Art's connection to an eighteen-year-old black girl is too compelling to ignore. I will take another crack at coming up with some answers.

"Cuppa's, this afternoon?" I finally agree.

I almost don't recognize her as I look around the coffee shop. Latisha has become a sleek, young woman since that late-night visit. Her shining hair is shoulder-length, very straight, held back by a small barrette on one side and by an ear, dangling a gold trinket, on the other.

"Like it?" Latisha grins. "It's my going-away present from Helen. I guess she was getting tired of me swishing my curls around while I ate my cereal in the morning."

Now that it's not overwhelmed by hair, her face emerges. Her eyes, soft brown, fringed in black, shine with good spirits. Latisha unzips her fleece coat. I have had the impression that she is heavyset, but as the jacket comes off, a slim, athletic body shows itself. I'm sitting across from a tall, budding beauty.

"Yes, I do like it. A lot." Then I can't help asking, though it's none of my business. "How did you get your hair to go that way?"

"Madame Lucy's wig shop." Again Latisha grins. "Me and Oprah, you know?"

No, I don't know. I suppose it's like wearing a new hat or maybe terrific shoes, and you feel like a changed woman. Maybe you are a changed woman. I've tried it, haven't I, to be changed? Going blond, new haircut. But a lot of other things have changed, too. Maybe it isn't just the hair—in either of our cases.

"How is everything going, Latisha? With school and work?" Without Art, I want to add but don't.

"Let's get some coffee, and then I'll tell you my good news." When we sit back down at our table, Latisha hasn't yet raised her cup when she says, "Guess what." Without waiting for a guess, she goes on, "I inherited some money. From a stranger who I never met. At least that's what the letter from the attorney says. College without having to work so much."

"The same person Art told you about, the friend who helped out with room and board at Helen's and tuition money for college?"

"I don't know. The attorney said she couldn't tell me who this person is, but that I'll get a check soon for first and last month rent and after that, a check to help with expenses every month. He knew my mother, my birth mother, a long time ago. I'm saying he but I don't really know if it is a man." Latisha catches her breath. "Can you imagine?"

Yes, I can. I eye the girl over the edge of my cup as I try not to choke the hot liquid draining into my throat. Art. Why? And How? Then I see it: the familiar cheekbones, the broad forehead, the small ears, the long body. Latisha looks like a young, brown, female Art. Is Art's child. That's why. Their meetings. The envelopes filled with bills. Somehow he'd gotten the money, managed to pass it on to a child he could never own up to. I should feel relieved, I suppose, to discover this truth, lover was a bit of a stretch I realized the moment I came up with that idea, but for some reason I'm filled with sadness. I manage to put my cup down.

"Have you thought that this person might have been my husband?"

Latisha doesn't answer right away. Her face is still, her eyes focus on her drink. "Yes, I thought maybe..." She raises her head, meets my eyes. "But I called, asked the lawyer. She said she couldn't identify who this person is.

"Why not?"

"She couldn't tell me anything more, she said. She'd probably said too much as it was. She told me to stop guessing and enjoy my good fortune." Her face brightens. "So I'm going to. I'm meeting my new roommate today, and we'll be fixing up a little apartment near school."

"Do you remember the attorney's name?"

"I think something like Jessica Stewart. She sounds nice over the phone. Said she specialized in estates and stuff like that."

"Your foster mom is okay with all this?"

"It's a relief for them. They need the income from having foster kids, and my official stipend stopped coming in on my eighteenth birthday. I'll still see them. And you, I hope. And Brody, of course."

I'm having trouble swallowing again, especially the assumption that the two of us will be friends, including my dog, even as Art's money is paying for Latisha's new life, despite what the lawyer claimed. A fund of some sort is handing out monthly allowances, maybe from our joint bank account, like paying the newspaper bill or my Visa charges. I probably would never have noticed. I've never been good about money, one of the reasons Art always managed ours. Art once again is in control of my purse.

I push back my chair. "I'm glad for you," I force myself to say. "Have fun fixing up your new home." Then I add, "I'll call you soon."

In four steps I am out of the door and out of that girl's life.

Especially after I call Herbert Smith, Art's attorney, and he denies knowing anything about Latisha, a monthly check, Jessica Stewart, or any sort of money arrangements except for the pension which he is assuming I am now receiving. He sounds annoyed, as if perhaps he should have known. I feel the same way. I choose to believe him.

20

The next morning Brody's tongue wakes me up from a strange dream that involves water running down the walls of what was once a lovely old home, mine perhaps, and I am crying and mopping up waterfalls cascading over a mantle and into the fireplace. I am glad Brody has saved me from whatever will happen next, even though the dream leaves me uneasy. "What was that all about, dog?" I ask as Brody makes his have-to-go pant at me. "A white wine funk, friend. Be glad you don't drink chardonnay."

I've just let him out when the phone rings and for a minute, still befogged by flowing water and remnants of last evening's anxiety, I don't want to answer it. I get to the phone by the fourth ring, and a voice I recognize greets me.

"Sergeant Durrell?"

"Yes." Once again the man seems to be eating while he is talking to me. I wait for him to swallow. "We just got a call from California Mutual. They are about to close the file on Art Finlay, but they have a question about the coroner's report."

So do I, I almost say, but I want to hear what the policeman has on his mind.

"What's the problem?"

"The coroner has ruled that the alcohol, Valium, barbiturate combination was not potent enough to cause death, and the insurance company is willing to accept that decision, but they are still questioning the atenolol prescription. The fact that it was never picked up at the pharmacy."

"How do they even know about it?"

Sergeant Durrell chews. "I may have mentioned it in my report—the empty container in the bag of vials you gave us that day. The coroner is questioning why the drug did not show up in the blood draw."

"Why?"

"From what I am told, stopping that drug abruptly can bring on a severe heart attack." I hear him swallow again, not going on with that thought. "Sorry."

"What does this mean?"

"The insurance company seems to be wondering if Mr. Finlay knowingly stopped taking the drug since suicide affects their pay out." Sergeant Durrell breathes into his phone. "It's kind of out of our hands, now. The coroner is not deciding on this one. You or the beneficiaries should be hearing from the insurance guy soon."

"Have you called to warn me...or out of duty?"

"Nah, it's my lunch hour. I just wanted you to know what's up. Good luck, Mrs. Finlay."

So maybe Art did choose pills to die, only too few, not too many. But what insurance policy is the policeman talking about? Sergeant Durrell has derailed my train of guilt thoughts, has sent me out on a familiar track of question marks. The first question follows last night's middle-of -the-night sleepless whirl of doubts: Eighteen years ago. What I remember about eighteen years ago is a stressful wedding that I had shamed Art into helping pay for. After that event, he sank even further into his doldrums, coming home, wading through his regular drink, the newspaper, and whatever television show he wanted to see each evening. The RV dream, the trip to all the national parks, drowned in dark mutterings about going broke on his government salary. He'd squint at me over the pile of bills, his eyes accusing me of killing an Airstream. He'd become a dreamless man; I can't imagine him opening up, caring for any another person. Unless she had six wheels, a pullout bed, and could take him far away from me. Perhaps he had found such a person, without the wheels, but with the power to take him away from his real life. I can't imagine what she might have seen in him. Eighteen years ago. Maybe. Maybe a remnant of the same sort of sexiness I once fell for in that backseat. The Daughter theory has become credible, and the similar cheekbones, the years of silence, resentment seem to add up. Lover, as complicated as that theory is, still lurks in the shadow as a possibility.

I take out Art's still-cluttered files. I've already received a settlement from Atlas, a company we insured with early on, on both of our lives, a term policy payable on death or, while we were still alive, at a smaller amount. Art refused to even consider using that money when we toyed with the dream of a beach cabin. California Mutual? I page through a handful of files looking for that logo, and have just about given up when I find it. A crisp folder, marked CM with a date, a date only four months ago.

Who can understand these things? I pour a glass of wine, early in the day but necessary, sit down, the file in my lap, and try. If I'm reading it correctly, Art took out an insurance policy for $400,000 on his own life last fall. Beneficiaries, plural, are Brian Finlay and Latisha Spencer. A handwritten note at the back of the folder says, "This is for all that you've done for me."

Latisha, for God's sake? Brian, his son, of course, but really, what had Brian ever done for his father except stay out of his way?

Brody has come to like the taste of my ankles, and I kick him away as I contemplate my dead husband. And the fact that one of the business cards in the manila folder is that of an insurance agent. Stephen Crandall.

A very insurance-y name. And an address and a telephone number. If the sergeant is correct, Stephen Crandall may be searching his files for a lost wife at this very moment. I go to the closet, take out my jacket. I'll beat him to the draw, ask him questions first. Like, just how did Art explain his need for this new policy, if he ever did?

The office is hunkered inside a mall on the second floor. Through the glass door, I can see a young woman-girl, behind the desk, talking on the phone. When I go in, she, Julie Abramovich, the plaque in front of her reads, raises her eyebrows in a hello and points at the phone, signaling with a swirling index finger pointed at an ear, a long, boring conversation. I choose one of the two black leather chairs and listen to the ums and ahhs sliding at me until the receptionist finally says, "I'll be sure to tell him, Mrs...." Julie looks down at a note in front of her, "Gadsby. I've written everything down, and he'll get back to you. Thanks for calling." She hangs up and rubs her ear. "Third time she's called this morning." Then she turns up the corners of her red lips and asks what she can do for me.

I will not explain a thing to Julie, who is obviously suffering from communication exhaustion. "I want to talk to Mr. Crandall about the policy my husband, Art Finlay, bought a few months ago. If he's busy, I'll wait."

Something I say has perked up the girl. She pushes a button, says, "Mr. Crandall, Mrs. Finlay is here to see you." For some reason she winks at me. "If you have a moment." When Mr. Crandall says yes, of course, Julie takes her finger off the intercom and explains, "We've been trying to get ahold of you. The phone number we have doesn't seem to exist." She waves a hand at a door in back of her. "Go right in."

I'm sure my phone exists. Didn't I just talk on it this morning? "What number?"

The girl flips through a couple of notes on her desk. "I have 289-4321. Not yours, I'm guessing."

"Probably no one's," I answer as I enter the room. Stephen Crandall, a thirtyish, young man with a sculptured beard and silk tie, is standing behind his desk, holding out his hand to me. I give it a twitch and pull the guest chair closer, so that I can put my purse on the desktop, a habit I am working on after leaving purses on the back of chairs once too often. "I know you want to talk to me," I say, hoping my voice is businesslike, whatever that is, "but first I need to get some information from you. I did not know until this morning that my husband bought a large insurance policy from you three months ago. I want to know the circumstances, how he explained his purchase to you, and how he paid for this policy. As you may know, he is dead."

Mr. Crandall settles back in his chair, adjusts something crotch-wise, and scowls at me. "Since your husband did not tell you about the policy, some of what you are asking me is privileged information, Mrs. Finlay. I am uncomfortable answering several of your questions, about our private conversa—"

"Uncomfortable!" Am I yelling? I take a breath, lower my voice. "Well, just get uncomfortable then. I am so uncomfortable I am planning on going to my lawyer, Seth Benjamin, and asking him to get a court order to force you to talk about your connection with my husband. I am, or was, his wife, forty-some years of being privy to all of his doings, and you are telling me you have a right to keep secrets from me now that he's dead?" I hope he won't look up Seth in the yellow pages, and yes, I did lie a little about being privy, but I can't stand the frown floating above those earnest, wide, insurance-man eyes.

He hesitates, rubs his ear. "Okay. But if I do tell you what you want to know, you will have to answer my questions."

Since I'm sure that I don't know much about Art, I agree.

A few hours later, I call and invite Lynne in for a glass of wine and a summary of my conversation with Stephen Crandall, a man who might be in trouble. She arrives carrying more wine and a sack of food. Brody is delighted to sample a new set of ankles. "Probably my new...lotion," Lynne says, giving the dog a couple of nudges with her foot. "A dog with discriminating taste. Wednesday/Saturday man likes it too."

We're steaming the half dozen tamales she picked up at Miguel's Mexican on her way to my house, and I wonder how one eats them. Certainly not the husks, I decide. Lynne will lead the way with the food; I'll do the same with my own contribution to the meal.

I pull my story into an understandable rant. I tell her how Art appeared at Stephen Crandall's office door a day after tucking the insurance man's card in his pocket. They had met at a restaurant. They both had younger women at their sides, and when Art's woman left, a black woman with big curly hair, he mentioned that he might need an insurance policy. The business talk sent Stephen's girl out the door also. The men agreed to meet the next day.

Art told him that he needed to take care of several people who were not on his term policy. He didn't want his wife to know, although she'd find out when the time came. He produced a medical report, dated a few days before, that stated he was in good health except the usual cholesterol problems of older men, for which he took medication. The report satisfied Stephen, and he didn't ask for a physical. They signed the policy, and Art made the first payment with a check. Next payments would be taken automatically out of his bank account monthly.

Lynne lifts her eyebrows and the lid to the steamer at the same time. "No physical?"

I go on with my story. "The agent hesitated, this time not looking at me as he explained that he had not called the doctor who had signed the report. Oversight. Probably because a policy that large doesn't walk in the door every day."

Lynne reaches for the wine bottle. "So he missed something important?"

"Yep. Like the beta blocker his doctor had put Art on months before. The doctor's report was an old one. Its date, according to Mr. Crandall, must have been changed because when he checked with Dr. Blakely after Art's autopsy report came in, atenolol was on the list of prescriptions."

"Atenolol? For blood pressure? So Mr. Crandall is feeling a little guilty—or maybe his company is requiring an explanation? Like maybe the meds might be involved in Art's death? Before it hands over $400,000? And he's asking you to help get him off the hook?"

"He was vague. He answered my questions about Art's reasons for getting a new policy by saying that Art told him he'd met someone he loved, and he needed to take care of her."

"The girl with big, black hair?"

"Seems so. Latisha. Art included Brian in the policy so we wouldn't protest, passive-aggressive to the end." A twinge of pain passes through my throat as I say this. It's hard to forgive when you're not sure what you are forgiving.

I sip my wine and decide to tell the rest, how when I had asked about Art's state of mind during all this, Mr. Crandall had twitched.

"Something else I missed," he said. "Art seemed quiet, depressed maybe, anxious to get it taken care of. Like…"

"Like he had a plan?"

The agent sat back. "If he did, I didn't suspect anything." He grimaced, looked at me. "I've told you what you want to know. Now it's your turn. When did you find out that Art was taking atenolol?"

"Never. Art and I never talked about it." But I did know about it, in a misplaced way. I didn't want to explain to this person who also has been lying to save his guilty skin. Like I was.

"You were married to him. How could you not know? My wife hands me my pills with a glass of water every morning."

"We didn't have that kind of marriage."

"And his being depressed? You knew?"

"Art Finlay was born depressed."

"Any different or strange behavior before his death?"

"He left sometimes in the evening, returned hours later, did not explain."

"And?"

I'd shared enough. "I never knew where he went. Like I said, we didn't have that kind of marriage. Maybe not a marriage at all." I stood, held out my hand to the insurance salesman, who, on reflex, took it. "I hope I helped you, Mr. Crandall. If you are wondering, I will not protest the policy's beneficiaries. And I truly don't know if Art somehow killed himself chemically. It's very unlikely, given his strong feelings for a young woman. If anyone, he probably wanted to kill me. You have my permission to convey that thought to your superior."

Then I tell Lynne what Sergeant Durrell told me about beta blockers, about stopping them, hinting that maybe Art stopped them on purpose, to send me, everyone, a message.

Lynne frowns. "It might have been a message to you, his wife. But what message would the girl get? No guy in the middle of a relationship, of whatever kind, with a willing young woman would want to die. Besides, Art wasn't that creative. If he had wanted to die, he would have made you so miserable you really would have killed him."

My friend is reading my mind again. Even she can imagine his empty-of-love wife willing him to die.

21

"How wrong can a person be, Brody? I have suspected that smiling girl of being his daughter. Now Stephen Crandall and Lynne believe she could have been his lover. Maybe I do too." We are eating breakfast, Brody chomping loudly, me stirring my coffee. When the door opens, I half expect Art to walk in, smelling like his other life. Instead, it is Kathleen, who hands me a bag of cinnamon apple turnovers and pours herself a cup of coffee.

"Got some time, Mom?" she asks.

Brody edges in on the bag being emptied and yips for us both.

Kathleen hesitates as she bites into a warm crust. "Do you know about the insurance policy Art took out?"

"Yes. I'm interested that you know, too."

"I'm now reading Brian's mail, along with a couple of other undercover activities. Apparently, he may receive $200,000, which is good, I guess. But who is this Latisha person?"

"Art's lover." When I say this out loud, I begin to accept the truth of it, the motivation fueling those late-night walks. Seems logical. A man, old, tired, probably sick, searching for one last reason to be alive, finds it in a lovely, joyful young woman who he knows will weep when he is gone—unlike the shrew he has lived with uncountable years, a woman who cannot find it within herself to even talk to him.

"Migod, Edith." No Mom here. Kathleen's not looking for help. "What do you mean? Art could hardly rouse himself to crawl out of his big chair. Lover?" Then she seems to reconsider what she's just said. "Oh." The turnover lies forgotten on her saucer.

"There were probably reasons." I don't tell her what's going through my mind because it feels too painfully true. Maybe the next time we talk. Instead I repeat what I've learned at the insurance office, including the fake telephone number Art used yet one more time, and when I finish, I change the subject.

I remember to ask, "So what about you?"

Kathleen shrugs. "Brian's being good with the kids and, I have to admit, really good with me. He still works late once in a while, and I am tempted to call the office. Usually, he calls me first. Maybe a husband having a secret lover isn't so bad for the wife." Then she grins, shakes her head. "Sorry. Secret lovers seem to be the theme of the day."

"Yep." I'm through trying to make sense of men, their vulnerable undersides when it comes to their penises and their unspoken hollow places. I am mostly, right now, glad that a daughter is sitting at the other side of the table and pouring each of us another cup of coffee. "When lovers aren't secret any more, a lot is explained."

"So what is there to do? What would you have done if you knew then what you think you know now about Art and the young woman with black hair?"

"I might have killed him, just for the pleasure."

Even before I knew about Latisha, I suspected that I had murdered him with deadly unlove, and I halt in mid-sentence and change the subject again. "Nothing I can do about it, is there? And you are satisfied with Brian's conversion to what seems mostly like old times?" We still have a mystery to solve if she's up to it. And I owe her, big time.

"I probably won't kill my husband while he's on this good-behavior binge, but what was that citrus smell all about? And the late nights? And why don't I trust him, really, even now? No, I've been investigating, like you. I've gotten quite good at it, still am, if you count opening envelopes and checking bank accounts daily. I have a few clues of my own. Are you up to a few visits to some places like to those we've already snooped in? I need a partner."

"Yes!" I need to be distracted from this over-whelming obsession about an unfathomable old man and his possible lover. With Brian, the mystery will be something managea-ble, all participants still alive, young, something to do with business, male menopause, an itch that needs to be scratched.

"Good. I'll come by tomorrow morning, after I take the kids to school."

I hope we don't find out anything terrible. Brian is still my son, and I'm not quite ready to find out that the perfect boy has gone bad.

Kathleen comes by at ten o'clock, and we go out to coffee to discuss our tactics. We will try to uncover a clue to wherever Brian has been going and to confront him. At least, Kathleen will do the confronting, that not being a mother-in-law's prerogative. Or a mother's.

"So what do you know?"

"That he sometimes had that strange smell. Other than that, my once-detective followed him to work, to the squash courts, to a bar, to a movie. One time he drove in a iffy neighborhood that my sleuth didn't follow him into, just waited until Brian's car emerged and headed home. I fired him when he couldn't tell me street names, only about the gangs he spotted on dark corners."

"Good riddance. Everyone has dark corners. And gangs of worries. He wasn't being paid to retreat from them. You and I aren't retreating, are we?"

"Not sure we're getting paid either." Kathleen grins.

"What about the bar? Could he come up with an address?"

"In the northeast, Boo's Soul. Brian and I have never gone there, so that may be the only mystery, except why he keeps coming home smelling like..."

"Oranges?" Way too many coincidences. I'm remembering again Art's alcoholic orangey smell on Christmas Eve .

Kathleen explains. "Once or twice, citrusy, maybe more like weed, lately."

"Weed, like home-on-a-Saturday-night weed?" I can imagine that. I've read about it, have given some thought to it, if I could figure out how to get it.

"We don't smoke it at home. The kids. Sometimes at parties, but not lately, not so that we come home exhaling cannabis."

I'm glad to hear that. "So your detective could not identify the source of the various smells?"

"He himself smelled. Beer. God, does a person have to do it all herself?"

Probably, I think. Who else is there "Boo's Soul. I know that place. Get a babysitter. We're going there for happy hour. A good plan," I assure Kathleen, "and our only clue."

Kathleen follows MiKaela to the table. Our server doesn't recognize me. Probably the blond hair, and the peel I managed to get yesterday morning, Phoenix squeezing me in between appointments saying, "At last. I've been waiting." My skin is a little red, still, but the age spots are almost gone. It's very ego-boosting to have them disappear, to not have to call them big freckles, not have to use Cover Girl to hide them along with the bags still blooming under my eyes. Definitely, a facelift when this is all over. I'm not sure when I will know it is all over, however. Right now, I am aware of a pair of green eyes at the bar smiling at me.

I wave. "My friend Seth," I explain as Kathleen follows the wiggle of my fingers. "He might be helpful."

Seth makes his way to our table. "I've been waiting a while to call you, but I still have your number. How are you? And have you solved the Art mystery?"

"Actually, Seth, we have another mystery. This is Kathleen, my daughter-in-law. She's trying to figure something out, and again the search has led us to this place. I thought of you." I've thought of Seth often, but this isn't the time to admit it. "It may have something to do with Art, or maybe not. May be just coincidence that her husband..."

"Your son?" Seth is tracking well.

"Yes, Brian, his name is, apparently has come here at least once. We're wondering if you might recognize him." I open my wallet to a college graduation picture of Brian. "This photo is old."

Seth holds the photo for a moment. "This is Art thirty years ago. I don't remember seeing a young Art lately. Around here, at least. I'll be at the bar. Drop by before you leave."

"And MiKaela?" I signal to the aproned woman looking this way from the other side of the room.

"Hi! Welcome back, Art's wife." MiKaela is back on track too, probably remembering the old lady who tips well.

"Do you recognize this person, only fifteen or more years older? Maybe without the longish hair? We're on another hunt for lost men." We snicker as if this is perfectly under-standable, and MiKaela squints at the photo. "Looks famil-iar. Not your Art, though. Too skinny." She frowns and adds, "A guy like him was here a while back. Real nice. The woman he was with was under the influence. He paid the bill, helped her out, and I guess he got her home since she wasn't outside when I left twenty minutes later. Nice guy, like I said, a little embarrassed." MiKaela glances at the ta-bles in her area. "I gotta go." She grins as she tucks her pad into her belt. "I love getting even with men."

As the waitress leaves, Kathleen asks, "Are we trying to get even?" She lifts her glass.

"Even would be good," I answer, pushing aside a few stomach-stirring thoughts of Seth, who has gone back to his stool at the bar.

"Has it ever been even?" Kathleen glances at her watch. It's time to get back to the kids so I don't answer.

At the door, we stop MiKaela as she balances a tray of drinks on one upraised arm. "So what did the person under the influence look like?"

I tuck a crumpled bill into her apron waistband, ala Kathleen, and I hear, "Drunk. Worn down, fortyish. African American. Really bad hair. That's all I can remember."

The two of us are in the car before either of us says any-thing. Kathleen breaks the silence. "I can't imagine your son with a woman with bad hair."

"No. I taught him better than that. Hair is important."

We go to Kathleen's house because the sitter needs to be home by seven and Brian has a meeting in Seaside, or at least says he does, Kathleen adds, opening the door. Winston and Meg call from the TV room as Sharon, the sitter, comes out, books and coat in hand.

"Thanks for getting here on time," she says, accepting the bills Kathleen counts out into her hand. "Big test tomorrow. Everybody ate their tomatoes and pizza. The broccoli didn't find any takers until I let them dip it in ranch."

"Yes, I know. I was hoping you'd have better luck than I. Good move with the ranch. See you again soon."

As Sharon closes the door behind her, I locate the children. A young singer with shoulder-length hair is a bigger attraction at the moment than a grandma. I look around the living room. This might be the first time I've been in this house without Brian at my side. I've never been asked to babysit here, always some Sharon or Laurie taking that job, and I've never felt comfortable just dropping by. Something about the angular lines of the furniture, the white walls holding the strange angular paintings, the absence of toys and a neat scatter of magazines in the main rooms giving notice to the organized life my son and his wife lead has made me uneasy about stopping by without an invitation.

"Come into the kitchen, Edith. The kids won't need me for a while. A cup of coffee?" Kathleen leads me through the central hall to the kitchen, whose windows look out on a misty green mound of dark hills. "This is my favorite place," she says. "Even in winter the light is wonderful here." She begins a pot of coffee while I find a chair at the kitchen table. Like I would at Lynne's, I think.

"I've always admired this house. So...clean, calm."

"So cold." Kathleen pushes the ON button on the coffee maker. "When Brian bought it five years ago, he had a vision of how he wanted live in it. I had no vision. I didn't even want a new house back then, just a place where we could both land every night, talk, and escape from our days. I was still working, the kids were little and in day care. His job was going well, you remember, but he said he wanted roots, like his parents, but different, of course. He hired a designer. I worked with her on this room and the garden. He fell in love with Eames and black leather. And oriental rugs. I fell in love with evening blooming primroses and Oregon grape. And my gorgeous stove. Then I lost my job and found out what living in a house like this is really like."

"It's really quite special, the art, the rugs..."

"No place to sit around in my nightgown and clip my toenails. Or eat popcorn or spill soda or lounge about reading murder mysteries and drinking box wine. A couple of years later, we added the TV room and that was more me than anyone else. Brian conceded that maybe he'd gone too far design-wise. We de-sanitized the white bedroom, got rid of the fourteen pillows the designer had piled at the head board, and added a wall of bookcases for the paperbacks I'd been collecting, waiting for a new career."

"God, where was I during all this time?"

"It was both of us, Edith. I was sure you didn't like me. Remember that day I had the neighbors and you and Art in for a barbeque, and Brian dropped the fish on the patio, and I yelled at him. You shook your head and walked out, dragging Art with you, as if I had committed a terrible crime. Other times..." Kathleen gets up, pours coffee into our mugs.

"I remember being upset at the fish episode, but I wasn't mad at you. I was astonished. That you could let Brian know exactly what was on your mind at that moment. I could not do that, ever, with Art. I left because I was crying. I didn't want to cry. Especially in your house."

"But, admit it, you never liked me, did you?"

"I guess what matters is that I like you now. I was a foolish woman consumed by jealousy that was gnawing on me one cell at a time. You were a perfect wife. I had become a Grimm's fairytale mother-in-law. You had the perfect husband, my son. I had..." I close my eyes, a sound heaves out of my throat that feels like a distant wail.

"Mom!" The table shakes as Kathleen pushes against it. She comes to my side, touches my shoulder. "It's okay, Edith."

Then I am blinded by two soft breasts pushing into my forehead, am deafened by a body wrapping around me. My hands reach out to hold the hips leaning into me. I don't know whether to laugh or to cry.

Winston decides for me.

"Mama, can we watch one more show? It's only eight thirty." He stands looking confused but hopeful at the doorway.

I lift my head, find my breath and my composure, and answer, "I'll read you both a story if you are in bed in fifteen minutes. And don't forget your teeth." I wipe my eyes on the lovely cloth napkin Kathleen had handed me with my coffee, and as the children go to their rooms, I laugh, "Thank you, daughter."

We'll talk about the drunk woman at Boo's Soul tomorrow, and maybe my swarm of Latisha guesses have been calmed for a while over a kitchen table.

22

The calm doesn't last long. The next morning I realize I need to talk to someone other than Brody. Kathleen is not answering her phone, probably out prowling the streets. I call Lynne.

"So, how're the new cheeks?"

"I haven't called Dr. Johansen yet. I will, later, when I solve a mystery. Have time to listen? No Thursday/Sunday guy? I can come over if you'll be home."

Sometimes I use the public transit to get places, but Lynne lives in a new part of town, across the river, and I don't know the bus routes. Going there by car requires feeding a parking meter. I drive over one of the five possible bridges, fortunately the one that leads to her condo. I find a parking place, and it takes me a few minutes to figure out

how to get my money into the machine, the first quarter
going into an abyss. I know I look like a senile old lady as I
squint at the instructions, and I hate that look. Especially
when I'm wearing it.

"How long you gonna be?" His smell precedes his words.
A grocery cart sidles up beside me and his stained fingers
reach out towards my change-filled hand. I look at him and
then down the street. This bearded man leaning on his plas-
tic-bag-stuffed grocery cart is the poster boy for street persons. Only his eyes seem okay, the rest of him stiff with oily
grime, the origin of the several layers clothing hanging off
his narrow shoulders unidentifiable. He wipes his hands
across his ragged beard. Except for the two of us, the sidewalk is empty. He grins, displays five-and a-half yellow
teeth. "I can help you."

He is one of the reasons I have never considered moving
into the center of the city. "Never mind. I can do it," I snap,
fumbling with the knobs on the meter.

"You just slide the coins into this place until you get
enough time." The man's not going to quit with his helping.
"Then you push this knob for the time to show. Try it. You
can do it." He pats my arm encouragingly.

Helpless, I do what he tells me to do. A moment later,
the paid time appears. "And?" I ask, hating myself for being
so embarrassingly dependent on this smelly Samaritan.

"You're good. Make sure you lock the car door."

I do, and he is still standing at the meter. "Thank you," I
say as I hand him the three quarters resting in my palm.

"Thank you, ma'am. Have a righteous day." He tips his nonexistent hat and walks away. He seems to be looking for other meter-challenged old ladies. It's probably a good business.

Lynne has been watching from her sixth-floor balcony, and when she answers the door, she says, "Hey! Should have brought him up. Looked like a good candidate for Thursday/Sunday."

We settle on the sofa, and Lynne takes out a cold bottle of chardonnay and two glasses. "You look good, blond. Keep going. A tuck here and there," and she pulls at the skin at her ear lobes, "and voila, fifty again." As she pours the wine, she asks, "So what's up?"

I haven't really looked at Lynne lately, too self-involved last time. I realize that Lynne's face isn't the same face she wore a few years ago. Something about the eyes. Where are the frown lines she's had from maybe when she was a baby? She seems a little shiny.

"I am shiny," Lynne says, apparently reading the look I've just given her, "because I had a little tuck or two myself, and my skin is still tight. Stays that way for a while and then loosens up. I'm ready, if that's why you are here, to offer advice on this sort of stuff." She glances at me, blinking her new eyelids and adds, "But that's not why you are here, is it?"

Thirty years later we still can read each other's minds. "No, but before I get into that..." I'm not quite ready to reveal it all, so I change the subject. "What ever happened to what's-his-name, the snowmobile guy?"

"Your snowmobile guy went into the Peace Corps after saving you from freezing to death with his hairy chest."

"Pardon me! As I recall, I saved him, with my fat boobs."

"And my snowmobile guy has been my Wednesday/Saturday guy ever since his divorce fifteen years ago. We kept in contact in the interim, even after he sold the snowmobile. He..." Lynne blushes. "He suits me, in the snow or not."

"No regrets?"

"None. How about you?"

I blink to clear up an unanticipated blurring of my left eye. "I need you to help me decide if I have regrets."

Lynne pours more chardonnay. "I have the time and the wine."

The telling takes an hour, words wandering, circling, capturing odd scenes, feelings, and the obsessive urgency of my search for truth in Art's pockets. Finally, the biggest mystery of all: I describe a girl with interchangeable hair who has somehow inherited money to go to school and start her life. "You wonder if I have regrets, Lynne. I do. Lots of them. But my biggest regret is that I never knew my husband. Ever." I put the napkin to work again.

Lynne is quiet for a moment, then she laughs, Lynne-like, "I didn't either. Of course, my husband was crazy. I just didn't know why. Nowadays it's said to be a matter of chemicals and genes. All I knew was that at times living with him was so exciting I didn't ever want it to stop. But the godawful times would descend like black angels, and then I'd blame myself for disappointing him, not believing enough in his wondrous schemes and ideas." She reaches for her glass. "Thank God that roller coaster has stopped." She settles back into the sofa, tucks her legs under her. "So is your roller coaster slowing down at all?"

"Brody helps keep me level, doing the day-to-day things one does when one looks out for someone else, including a dog. He understands me, my moods. The other night I was huddled in the corner of the sofa, eyes closed, deep into one of those funks fueled by self-pity, when I felt him jump up next to me. He edged in, sighed once or twice, and then leaned into my body." I reach for my wadded napkin; this time the tears make it to my nostrils. "How did he know how sad I was?"

"That's what friends do. You're lucky to have him. I have a turtle that I mostly keep in a box for my two grand-kids. Not quite the same, although he does come for lettuce when I open the fridge door. Which reminds me, how about a frozen pizza?"

"My parking? I only paid for two hours."

"Not to worry. The old guy you already met? He patrols the parked cars, and if he sees the meter reader coming on her bike, he plugs a quarter or two in any delinquent meters. If he's leaning against your fender when you go out, you owe him a few bucks. He's not a bad guy."

"He really smells.

"Yeah, well, you can't have everything."

So Lynne takes in the details of my recent life, offers piz-za, and for some reason, I feel a lot better. It could be the wine, but it's more like knowing someone else doesn't believe I'm crazy, when I myself have doubts.

"I'll tell you what I think," she says, poking a crust into her mouth and pausing to chew. "I have a different theory. I think that your former husband had an attack of conscience, maybe about the time his doctor told him to do something about his high blood pressure, and he went searching for his lady friend of twenty years ago and found instead an eighteen-year-old young woman who looks a little like him only browner. When he finds her, he gets to know her and decides to make up for whatever happened before she was born. And maybe after. Thus the college money when he died, the other money before. Your dead husband may be proving himself to be an honorable man, even if doing so leaves you in the dark."

Of course, as I guessed, his child. Another lover, yes, but years ago, maybe before the loan to Brian, the twelve-hour days. Makes more sense than imagining Art in bed with an eighteen year old. But this explanation seems faulty, too. I have trouble seeing Art as honorable, especially as an honorable father. I don't feel any better.

"Why do I feel so guilty?" I ask my friend who is looking very pleased because she's cracked the nut and found the kernel of truth in my story.

"Guilt is toxic. Get rid of it. The two of you married, had a great kid, kept a sane house, usually, and were a committed couple in the eyes of the world, if not in reality, except for maybe a brief time in the middle. Not your fault, damn it." Lynne is getting worked up and she reaches into the freezer takes out our dessert, two frozen Dove bars. "Why do women always believe it's our fault?"

Lynne chomps down on her ice cream as if she believes that it is the bar's fault, all this guilt, all this angst.

"Because maybe Art killed himself." That's what I'm feeling guilty about, not the girl, not some fling that tossed a child into an unfair world. Maybe it's the coroner's report about barbiturates and Valium, or the vials labeled Lipitor, but the mystery that sticks in my craw is the detective's interest in the missing atenolol. Somehow, could it have led to his death as I slept beside him? A death he organized?

"So what?" Lynne stands up, makes her way to the shelf holding a bottle of Courvoisier, and comes back with two crystal liqueur glasses. "If he did himself in, it was his choice, wasn't it?"

She pours and hands a glass to me. "If I were you, knowing who you used to be and who you are now, I'd say it is time to celebrate. To your new you."

As I'm sipping the brandy, I understand one thing. I am responsible for Art's death. He had a secret he couldn't tell me, a lost love child, a secret that weighed on him for years until he went out to find her. He did, even though all he could do was meet her, give her money, continue to keep her a secret. He knew I would never accept the girl, forgive him his moments of escape from me, allow a black sister to join our son. I had never forgiven him for anything, ever. I had never forgiven him for being who he was, a sad, hard-working man captured in a joyless marriage.

NEVER TOO LATE

I don't say any of this to Lynne. She is celebrating the new me and doesn't want to hear the old me's truth.

23

I am standing on one shaky foot, the other hanging out behind me as I lean into the top of the wooden ladder. I take a handful of drape, dust flying, and give it a yank. The fabric, rod, screws, fall at me. I am wrapped in faded philodendrons as I creep down the ladder, find the floor with a foot, then two, and relieve myself of the pile of cloth wound around my head and shoulders. It feels symbolic, this unburdening. Lighter physically and in spirit, I kick the mound of bad taste toward the bag heading for Goodwill.

When I came in last night, I saw what was wrong with my living room, if not my life, why it has been irritating me for a long time.

We bought this 1930's bungalow about the time Art became a secure government employee and the other dreams had settled down. Our son needed roots, a good school. I needed a front porch and a garden. Art, I'm not sure what he needed, but he knew a good bargain when he saw one: a house with a new furnace, storm windows, a forty-year roof and elderly owners eager to negotiate and move on. We got our loan and a womb of a home: warmed with dark woodwork, three-dimensional tiles depicting forest scenes at the corners of the wood-burning fireplace, and shiny maroon tile in the one-and-a-half bathrooms. The kitchen had been recently renovated. Its painted cabinets and olive green refrigerator glowed. The house was perfect—except for a constantly overflowing toilet in the small bathroom and the raccoons in the back wall. The stained glass windows on each side of the fireplace made up for these shortcomings. In my mind, at least.

Over the years, in thrusts of decorating, I have hung photos, postured blown glass creatures, arranged silk flowers and carved birds, and poked ostrich feathers in tall vases which I stuck in corners when it became obvious that they were too flamboyant for the maple coffee table.

After experiencing the pleasant calm of Kathleen's house, I opened my front door, switched on the light, and I knew what I had to do.

"Brody," I say as I take out a box of garbage bags, "we're going to get rid of The Stuff. You can help by not wandering around wondering what's happening. Yes, you may lie on the sofa. For today."

At the moment, Brody is growling at the hump of drapes. "It's okay, dog. Just get your body out of the way of my feet." I remove the hooks, toss them in the box on the table, then shorten the rod, wipe off the plastery screws, capture the odds and ends falling to the floor, and put the whole mess in a big black bag.

"Bag #1," I announce to Brody, who by now has taken me up on the offer of the sofa and lies napping on it.

Bags #1 through #5, and box A and B lean against the walls of the entry by lunchtime. I have had several moments of regret: the porcelain figurines, gifts from an aunt long dead and forgotten, the Japanese doll in the glass case, my mother's crocheted doilies imprinted with years of lamps and stained by coffee cups. Each item makes me pause before I put it in a box. But only the things from my grandmother, handed on by my mother, the china cup and saucer, the three too-precious-to-use green and gold relish dishes, the one unchipped dessert plate from an ancient trousseau, remain after I have gone through the buffet and closets.

The two rooms look as if they are waiting for what will come next: fresh flowers on the coffee table, new white lamps on the end tables, and a mirror instead of the orange and brown fall landscape print that has graced the fireplace for years. I rip up a corner of the wall-to-wall carpet, a once-tan now a mousey-gray mat, and see that under that carpet are old oak floors, once considered valuable and, if I'm guessing right, considering Brian's lovely floors, valuable again. I find a tablet, begin to make a list, know I am in deep trouble when I get to "14: A new dining room set."

I call Lynne.

"Sorry, sweetie. I'll call you back tomorrow. Wednesday, you know."

I call Kathleen. We haven't finished with the mystery of Brian and the woman with bad hair. Maybe neither of us wants to right now. The warmth of that last night still lingers. Maybe that's why I'm allowing old drapes to distract me. She doesn't answer. Perhaps she's distracted too.

I call Goodwill. They will pick up if there is enough stuff. So I throw in a bedstead, and the appointment person says they'll come with their truck tomorrow. Then I call Brian at work.

"I'm doing over a couple of rooms in the house. I don't have a clue, but I know, after seeing what you've done in your house, that you might have a few ideas." If we're ever going to talk about what's going on with him, we'll have to have a less stressful talk, as if I don't know a thing about anything. I must be patient about asking why he came home smelling like oranges just like his father.

I hear him breathe a ha as if he's relieved about something, the sound apparently a genetic tic. Maybe the orange scent is also. "Good. Kathleen said you two had been talking more lately. I'll drop by."

"On your way home from the office tonight?"

Winston has a basketball game at seven, so Brian is at my door at six. When he walks in, I see that he's lost weight, has gained tiny lines at the corners of his eyes. He looks older. Maybe I just haven't noticed before, but in this thinner state, he looks a lot like Art, when Art still seemed glad to be coming home.

"Nothing grand," I say. "Just a makeover for the life Brody and I'll be having here. I don't want always to be looking back." I hesitate but keep going. "I want to look forward to a new me and a new..." I can't come up with a word that will say what I mean. One that won't negate the good years I spent with this son in this house with its doilies and porcelain ladies "...a new environment." Then I understand. "You did the same thing, didn't you, with your white, clean, straight-edged house?"

"Only, if you ask Kathleen, and maybe you did, she'd say I went a few steps too far in my new environment. Did you notice the children's drawings hanging in the dining room? Her idea, and they perfectly break up the perfection I thought I wanted." Brian goes quiet for a moment. "Everyone seeks some kind of perfection, but perfection is always nudged into a different shape by contact with reality." He has shrugged off his suit jacket and plunges onto the sofa just like he did thirty years earlier, one foot on the cushions beside him. "So where are the ostrich feathers?"

We talk; he gives me the name of the designer he worked with. I won't go that far, outside help, but I am glad that he understands my need to give the house a facelift. I try to go a little deeper. How does he feel about a lift of my face?

My son's smile is the one I remember from years ago, sweet, tentative. "You are beautiful to me, Mom. But if you feel that removing a few wrinkles and bags, along with a Japanese doll and a couple of porcelain dancers, will make life easier, do it. Not for me and not for anyone who knows who you really are and loves you for it. Or despite it," he adds, teasing in his old way. "Just do what you want to do. You can do it now."

Brian, the witness to more than forty years of my marriage, is giving me permission to move on. Just as I am about to say more, to ask him to tell me what he looks forward to, to perhaps open up these past few secret months, he stands, pulls on his jacket, and heads for the door. "Winston is expecting me to show up at the game and yell myself red-faced in a few minutes."

He turns back, his eyes solemn, and he hugs me as I stand at the door. "It's going to be okay, Mom."

Which "it's" is he talking about? I wonder.

Brody grins and licks my ankle. "I know, dog. You want out. How about taking your own plastic bag with you and pick up your own stuff, like I'm doing around here?"

When we get back from our walk, and I'm frying an egg for a sandwich, I notice the message light flashing on the kitchen phone.

"It's Seth Benjamin. From Boo's Soul. I said I'd call, and I am. I'd like to see you again." He gives his number and I hit SAVE, since I have a spatula instead of a pencil in my hand.

24

"Your daughter-in-law came by again. Don't believe we helped her much. But that's not why I called." Seth pauses, seems to be taking a breath. "I'd like to take you to dinner, at a quiet place where we could talk, get to know each other. If it isn't too soon?"

He means, I know, after Art's death. Not soon enough, maybe, I'd like to answer. Instead I offer an "I'd like that."

"Is tomorrow okay? Maybe the Hilton?" What is it with the Hilton? Rendezvous Center? Maybe the rooms are cheaper than at the Heathman. Art must have known.

"That's fine," I say. "I'll meet you there at seven?" Seven seems like a sophisticated time, just beyond the happy hour. I can still get home by nine, in my own car. I read somewhere, probably in one of those magazines at the dentist's, that on a first date it is important to have your own car.

"Of course. Meet you in the bar."

We hang up. My fingers, reaching for a coffee cup, feel as if they're made of silly putty. I choose a wine glass instead. Thank goddess for chardonnay.

I have tomorrow to catch up with Kathleen. She answers when I call an hour later, and the soccer game must be over because she doesn't say much, only to say she'll come by in the morning if I want to go on a walk.

Brody and I do.

Kathleen strides briskly, talks briskly, and I find myself nearly strangling a meandering dog in order to keep up. "I've been very depressed," she says. "My doctor gave me a month's supply of Prozac, low dose, and after two days, I was nauseated, had a headache, and wanted to sleep all day. I knew I had to get off of it and face my problems head on."

"Sounds good," I pant, tugging at the leash. "Difficult sometimes, though."

"Well, yesterday morning I woke up as Brian was leaving for work, and I could hardly pull myself out of bed. I always make coffee before I read the paper and the kids wake up, and for some reason I looked at the Starbucks bag. Decaffeinated. I'd been in withdrawal for four days."

"Addicted." Brody has forced us to stop, and I hunt in my pocket for the plastic poop bag.

"Yes! I went across the street, borrowed a cup of coffee from my neighbor and in fifteen minutes, I was cured.

That's when I decided to return to Boo's Soul. And ask again about Brian. No one else recognized him. No orange smell, just catfish."

"Are you depressed again?" The coffee must be wearing off. Both Brody and I saunter beside her, matching her slowing pace.

"No. I've stayed on the Prozac. It seems to be working a little. Maybe more than a little. I'm considering telling Brian to go to hell, of leaving him."

All three of us come to a sudden stop.

"Is that the Prozac speaking?"

"No, it's the newest withdrawal from our retirement account. A phone call yesterday informed me that the check was ready. $15,000. I confronted him and he said—"

"'It's going to be okay.' He said the same thing to me."

"Is he on cocaine or something? Damn, if I can get crazy over caffeine, I can only imagine how screwed up a person could get on crack."

"I can't imagine Brian using drugs. Even the marijuana revelation was a surprise to me." My son. My husband. Valium, barbiturates, who knows what else? I look at the woman at my side wiping the sweat off her forehead with a kerchief, and I know that wanting to leave her marriage isn't because of the medication. She wants to escape a broken dream. I know about that. I just never had the courage to do it. My daughter-in-law does. "Don't decide for a while," I say. A painful surge fills my chest, tightens my throat— regret for my years of not knowing Kathleen and my grief for my son, in the midst of his own broken dream of some sort, the one that has led to mistakes, to his wife's decision. I can't bear to lose either of them. I touch her sleeve, say, "And if you do leave, I'll still want to walk with you."

We continue on, not talking, waiting for Brody to smell the trees, waiting for whatever will come next to both of us.

Finally, I can't stand the silence. And I'm sure my daughter- in-law is not ready to deal with my confused anxiety about Art and a black-haired girl. A person has to choose the best times to dump on a sympathetic friend. This is not one of those times. I will move away from my morbid obsession and onto something more positive, for both of our sakes. "I have a date," I announce as we stop for a red light to turn green. "With a man you met at Boo's. Seth."

The sign says Walk, but we don't step off the curb. "A date? With that handsome man with the green eyes?" And then she adds, "He called you?"

"As incredible as that seems, he did. Tonight I meet him at the Hilton bar, dinner." Kathleen stands, eyes wide, beside me. "He probably hasn't gotten a room, though. Seems a little soon," I add.

Her "Damn!" scares Brody back onto the curb. "So what are you going to wear?"

Other things on my mind, I've given little thought to that question. I have one short black dress, one pair of two-inch heels, and really fat knees. I noticed the knees lately when I convinced myself I should look in the full mirror on the back of the bathroom door. Are fat knees a common complaint of older women, even those like me who have managed to stay within ten pounds of their high school weight? I haven't seen any diets or any exercise routines that worked on fat knees. Bad knees, of course, which may also be fat, but my knees are still working pretty well.

"I'm pulled out a black dress I've had for years. It hits me right here, though." I pull up my pant leg, draw a line across my left patella. "Not my best feature."

I avoid looking at Kathleen's bony knees, very evident in the walking shorts she's wearing. I'd give anything for knees like that. And boobs like that. And the barely etched skin at the edges of the eyes that are now grinning at me. "He's not going to be looking at your knees, Edith. I've got a skirt that will solve that. And I've got some other tricks that will allow him to look into your soul."

"Is that good?

"It is, when the window is mascaraed, brown eyes floating in a lake of subtle sunset. Can you see anything without your glasses?" She doesn't wait for an answer. "If you need them, we'll just enhance the eyelids even more. We can do this. Knees don't count. Eyes do."

She seems as eager as I am to move out of our funk, at least temporarily. She'll come by in the afternoon and bring her supplies. I am to wash my blond hair and try to blow dry it upright, sexily boyish. I don't have a blow dryer, so she'll bring some product. I have product, I say, defending my stance as someone who knows a thing or two about new trends in beautification. When we say, "Later," we are chuckling, our quiet gasps like small suns lighting the dark clouds gathering on each of our horizons .

25

The Hilton restaurant is nice. Tablecloths, napkins, flowers, good silver. I turn a fork over and try to read the hallmark, but I'll need my glasses for that, and they are in my purse, waiting for the menu-moment. Seth has a very comforting face. I've seen eyes like his on another person recently. I don't want to remember whose.

"I'm so glad you agreed to see me, Edith. You and I have a lot to talk about. We barely know each other, but for some reason, I feel close to you." Because of those green irises, I choose to believe him.

I try to bat my eyes at him, but I keep getting an image of Mildred at the Metrobar and her false eyelashes slipping towards her cheek. I'm not wearing eyelashes, but I do have a generous supply of mascara weighing heavy along my upper lids, in addition to a color called violet passion that Kathleen said was perfect with my brown eyes. I had looked at myself after I put my glasses on, and I agreed I did look pretty good. This might be my first and my last date, but my daily routine in front of a mirror has been totally reorganized. I have product for my face now. Who knows what's next?

He's saying something. I focus at his mouth instead of his eyes. His smile reveals a slip of gold at the corner of his lip. "We have a friend in common, you know. Actually, my sister. You and she talked a while back? Social worker?"

The other set of green eyes. "Of course. She's been helpful during this whole Art thing. Did she tell you?"

Seth shakes his head. "She doesn't talk about her work much, but when I mentioned this determined woman out to find her dead husband Art, she nodded, said she'd talked with you."

I am not about to tell him anything more about my search. I'd like to forget it at least for a night. "And what do you do, Seth, besides buy drinks for women on quests?'

By now the waitress has brought our wine and stands waiting to tell us about the specials. We order, and I don't bother to look at the menu, just say "I'll have the same," and I wait for his answer. I hope what he says isn't too shocking.

It is, sort of. "I used to be an attorney with a good firm here in town. After thirty years, I figured I needed a break and I bought Boo's Soul. I needed to get back to my roots, I guess, and it was smoked ribs and the neighborhood from then on. That's about it.''

From the courtroom to the barbeque pit. There's got to be more. "No, it's not," I say. "You are or were married. You probably have grown kids now who don't do barbeque so much anymore?" I take a sip of my white wine and hope I've not said anything rude. I need to know this information before his fascinating eyes overwhelm me, and I don't give a shit about any of it.

"Was married, for a while. She was younger than me, just out of college." Seth shrugs. "It wasn't a good fit. We both knew it and after a couple of years, we understood we had to end it. We did. She went on to remarry, have children. I did not."

A drift of sadness makes its way between his words. I wonder what that is about, make another intrusive comment. "Was she pregnant when you got married?"

He moves his glass toward his lips, said, "Yes. How did you know?"

"I didn't."

"And you were pregnant when you married?"

I almost snort. "Of course. Why else would I have stayed with a man who didn't love me? You escaped." I don't mean escape, really, maybe more like found a way out. "How?"

Seth, the unfrownable person, frowns. "I've never talked about any of this."

I have overstepped. "You're right. It's not my business."

"No, it's not, and I want you to know. Janelle had a miscarriage during the fifth month. It threw us into a terrible

place. We were both gobsmacked by our loss. By the time
we had stored the bassinet and the playpen and given away
the onesies, we knew whatever we had felt for each other at
the beginning was gone. We divorced, but we've remained
friendly in a distanced way."

Over our pear salads, I wonder if I will ever be able to
say I am friendly in any way with the memory of Art. That
would take forgiveness and my supply of forgiveness is about
used up, although I have managed to forgive Kathleen for all
of her annoying take-over tactics. I admire them now. Arms
across her chest, feet firmly planted in her own sense of self,
she'll do something about Brian's wanderings. "And now
you're a happy person?" I ask.

The frown dissolves. "As happy as most folks, I guess."

I have nothing more to ask.

"And how about you? Are you a happy person?"

The waitress takes my salad plate away. I'm glad for the
interruption to consider this question, to realize I have an
answer. "I'm very happy at this moment. I have swells of
joy these days. I also have dark periods in which I question
if what I've done with my life is of any value. My son, my
one accomplishment, is on some mysterious path, my husband has left me wandering along a trail of guilt that
doesn't seem to have an end." I lift my glass, give myself a
moment to gather my thoughts. "My grandchildren now can
cook mac and cheese, my dog Brody speaks dog to me, my
friend Lynne makes me laugh." I realize I'm speaking my
truths to a man I hardly know. "I'm getting to be okay."

I am also aware that Seth is holding my free hand. "Yes, you are," he says. His fingers loosen. "Edith, this may be a deal breaker, but I've got to tell you something before this goes any further."

I feel my ribs squeeze, my breath can't find my lungs. "Okay." Better now than later. Isn't this what I want? No secrets?

Seth looks away, then back at me. "I know a little about Latisha and Art. I've suspected that he might be her father or something else, and I couldn't tell you when we first talked; you seemed too vulnerable." He revises that comment. "Not vulnerable, determined, I realized. Art introduced her to me, and I watched him talk with her over their barbeques, give her money, take her by the arm to his car, joke with her."

He continues, his words coming slowly. "I had to throw Latisha's mother out of Boo's a while back because she was so out of it that she was approaching every man with a proposition, loud, lewd."

"How did you know it was her mother?"

"Once when Patsy, who came by the bar often, was so drunk she didn't make sense, she told me that she'd had a child with a white man who had abandoned her when she told him she was pregnant. She'd given the baby the father's last name, called her Latisha, and declared that somehow, she'd find both him and her and get them both back. I suppose the last name was changed when the girl was adopted."

"Latisha." I tried it out "Latisha Finlay."

"You've met her?"

Will Art never let go of me? Or I him? Even as I allow myself to start to believe I can move on, begin a new life, maybe even one including a new man, that old man sneaks in, curls a lip, blows a ha across the table and I hear it.

My chanterelles in cream sauce look like vomit.

My fingers press against the saliva gathering in my mouth. I say, "Thank you for the nice evening." I manage to stand up, leave the table. Out on the sidewalk, still nauseous, I realize I've left my purse hanging over the chair back. I will not slink back in to retrieve it, but I have no car keys and no money for the light rail, and no money for the taxi driver holding a door open for me at the curb. I give him my son's address. When we get to Kathleen and Brian's house, the windows are dark. No one answers the door.

I send the taxi to my house because I must have some cash somewhere. I find my extra key under the fake rock, enter, go to the den and find it. A twenty-dollar bill with a telephone number on it. As I give it to the driver, I realize there is some kind of story here: the tale of a piece of paper passing between eager hands, distributing small rewards in its travels, to people who will never meet except in moments like this one. The driver nods at me, pulls away. Bon voyage, I think, and I open my front door. The end of this story eludes me, but I'm grateful that the crumpled twenty dollar bill and its ball-pointed message have passed on to its next owner.

26

"So how was it?" Kathleen calls early the next morning.

"I left my purse at the restaurant." Other than that bad news, I'm not sure how to answer. "He seems like a nice person," I finally admit, "but not much of a chance that it will go anywhere and probably shouldn't." I don't say any more, and Kathleen doesn't probe.

"Call the restaurant, they'll have it. You never know about the rest. Give it a little time." She has something else on her mind. "I have done something I'm not sure I should have, but I did. I am going to go through with it. I have an appointment with a divorce attorney."

I'm not like Kathleen. I probe. "What happened?"

"He's refusing to tell me what has been going on. The $15,000 was the last straw. Every time I look at him I wonder who he's been with, spending money on, maybe loving so much he doesn't care what I suspect. When I married him, I thought of him as a strong, ethical man with so much potential to do whatever he chose. Well, he's making choices now that makes me believe he might be crazy. I don't want to be married to a crazy person."

I can relate to that. But I can't to think of my son as crazy. A little stressed by something right now, a lot stressed, maybe. Stressed enough to make a couple of bad decisions. Really bad. I tighten my bathrobe belt and sit down. "I don't want to divorce you, Kathleen," I say.

"Mom, that won't happen. We'll still go on walks together, talk about the mysteries of Art and Brian over drinks, watch the kids grow up. Just not together as we'd planned. Maybe not on Christmas Day."

I should be relieved about Christmas Day. Instead, I find the words I need. It's time to give my blessing to my daughter-in-law. "Whatever you choose to do, I will support you." I lean back, look out the window. "I never had a choice, you know."

It is Kathleen's turn to be silent. Then she says, "I know. Thank you."

We have to move on, or we'll both be in tears. "So, how are the kids? Happy that spring break will be coming soon?"

Kathleen seems eager to change the subject too. "The kids—Winston is excited about soccer about to start. We have bought his shin guards and shoes, and he's signed up on his team from last year, the Bulls, only the team has girls on it now, and the girls want to call it the Bullettes. They're negotiating right now with the coach at school." Her voice changes as stress seeps into her words. "Meg, she...she doesn't want to go to school. Ever since winter break, she's been claiming she's sick, clings to me when I drop her off. She's even called from school begging for me to come pick her up."

"Teacher?"

"One of the best, a sensible, good-humored woman with a knack of keeping seven-year-olds in their seats and eager to learn what's next. Mrs. Williams doesn't know what's happening with Meg. Nothing negative in class; she has friends, she's capable and seems okay once we get her in the room." Kathleen takes a sip of whatever she's drinking, the glass clicking against the mouthpiece. "Getting her in there is the problem. She cries every morning, kids staring at her, as I yank her down the hallway to her classroom. When we get to the door, she grabs my leg, starts howling that she won't go in. Sometimes I can't get her through the door. Edith, she's missed all or part of five days in the last two weeks. I want to talk to the school counselor, but she's only there one day a week."

"The girl knows. Meg knows."

"What do you mean?"

"She knows that her home is changing. She's frightened."

"I don't understand. I haven't said a word to the kids. And God, she's only seven; she can't possibly know what I'm planning, or what Brian is doing."

"Her father knew. He was six. I had to drag him into his classroom, leave him wailing and clutching at me. 'Don't go,

Mama,' he'd scream as I shut the door. After a week of this, the teacher instructed me to leave and not to check back in or look through the window, just leave. He finally calmed down. But not before I assured him that no matter what he was worried about, I would never, never leave him. I'd always be there when he came home from school. Miss Fitzgibbons told me to say that every morning. School phobia, she called it. She'd seen it before. Something must be happening at home, she said. He's afraid to leave the house."

"And?"

I get up, tuck the phone under my chin, pour a cup of coffee. "Something was happening at home. One night, after a string of arguments over a couple of weeks, Art yelled at me, said terrible things. I yelled terrible things back at him. Art walked out. I ended up with bruises on my arms, crying on the front steps." I take a sip; an almost-lost memory slides through me. "I thought Brian had slept through it all. Apparently he hadn't, and it took an aging, spinster school teacher to figure it out."

I hear Kathleen breathe. "Her grandfather has died. Meg has heard our raised voices behind a bedroom door more than once. I've been distracted, not really there, even when my body is. Meg's afraid of being abandoned, isn't she?" A light chuckle of relief inserts itself between her words. "Thank God for aging spinster school teachers. And for you, Mom." I can imagine Kathleen squaring her shoulders. "I can do this, and so can Meg. I'll call her teacher this evening, tell her what you've said, what we both should do help a little girl to not be frightened anymore."

The dog is at the door, glancing back at me, waiting. "And let her know that Brody misses her. When she feels like it, we can do a sleepover, and she can bring a friend she wants. The dog will love popcorn." I try to remember where I've put the popcorn popper.

Kathleen murmurs a thank you and hangs up. It might be in the genes, like everything else, this phobia business. A little like this family's problem with males who smell like oranges. Will this ever end? This scent of unfaithfulness, the frightened eyes of children, the roar of divorce, the ever-present rumble of the one that never quite happened?

"Walk, Brody. A long walk. Somewhere along the way remind me to go and rescue my purse and the car."

27

Brian falls onto the sofa, and as usual, stretches out a leg. I have to stop myself from telling him to take his jacket off because I had the heat on, like I used to as his mother. He closes his eyes and seems to be gathering his thoughts. Maybe the "it's" that he assured is going to be all right, isn't.

"What?" I ask.

He sits up, props his elbows on his knees, his fists knotted under his chin. "Mom, I've got to tell you something, something that will shock you, something I've not been able to tell Kathleen, yet." He pauses. "You might need a drink before I'm through. I know I will."

It's still morning. I've never drunk alcohol in the morning, and my drug of choice is white wine. However, this seems to be a Scotch moment, morning or not. I find Art's unfinished bottle in the back of the cupboard, one of several artifacts I'd forgotten about, and bring it back to the living room. The cubes rattle in the two glasses I set on the coffee table. I pour the yellow liquid, its smell almost nauseating me.

"I know how Dad got the pills they discovered in the autopsy. No matter what the insurance company might conjecture, he didn't try to commit suicide with those pills." Brian raises the glass to his lips. "It's a long story."

I'm not sure I'm breathing.

"Couple of months ago, I asked Dad to advise me in a situation that had come up involving a woman I knew before I married Kathleen. A woman from my office. Guess maybe I was having cold feet about getting married. Whatever, she and I had a brief fling a few weeks before the wedding. I forgot about it until three months later when the woman told me she was pregnant. When I offered to pay for an abortion, she said that several of her friends had very bad experiences, and she was frightened by the idea. But she did want to quit her job so that no one in the office would know, and she needed money to live on until the child was adopted."

"What did Kathleen do?" I can't imagine Kathleen understanding a fling like this one. I don't understand it either. Brian? A man, if there ever was one. I have been so naïve, believing in flingless men.

"I didn't tell her. I sold some stocks, set up Patsy in an apartment, and when the child, a girl, was born, she was adopted. I didn't see Patsy for eight years, although she asked for a job reference once and seemed to be doing okay.

"Patsy." Seth's Patsy? "And by then you and Kathleen were also doing okay?" I ask. "Both of you with good jobs, planning a new house, and Winston?"

"He'd just been born when Patsy called me at the office, said she needed to see me. I met her in my car in a crummy part of town where she had a small apartment. She had become a druggie, her skin dry, her hair uncombed, her body too thin, boney. Only her gray eyes seemed the same. She'd fallen on hard times, she said. She needed to go to rehab, a good one, and get her life in order. She needed money to do it. If I didn't help her, she would go to my wife, tell her I had a daughter living somewhere close by."

I recall Kathleen after Winston's birth, postpartum big time. "You couldn't lay that on a weeping wife, could you?"

"No. I took four thousand out of the savings account and warned Patsy, 'Never again, ever.' Kathleen wasn't paying much attention to anything but Winston at that point and didn't notice the withdrawal. When I called the clinic after a month or so, they told me Patsy had completed treatment, and I was so relieved I didn't ask if they knew of her whereabouts. I just put the whole thing away for the next eight years."

Good years, I remember. Brian had started his own consulting firm, expanded it, became respected in business and government circles, and he had joined several prestigious boards. He'd built a house, had another child. Kathleen searched designer shops for outfits to wear to the occasional charity affair they were expected to attend. I was very proud of my son, but Art had worn his resentment of Brian's success like a barbed-wire cloak. He couldn't bring himself to do more than give his son a weak pat and a word, "Congrats," or "Great," at each revelation of good news. I wondered as I observed his tepid responses if he blamed this unplanned son, and that son's mother, for his own disappointment in the way his life had gone. Probably, I decided.

"Then?" I urge.

Brian runs his fingers over the top of his head, another of his father's gestures. His glance skitters across the ceiling before he answers. Then he tells how a few months ago he heard a noise, looked out the living room window and saw a woman reeling about in the driveway. Patsy. He went out, realized she was drunk, and he shoved her into the car, and called to Kathleen, who was watching from the doorway, that he was taking her to the police station. Once inside the car, Patsy grabbed his wrist, told she had something to show him at her apartment. Something very important to his future. He followed her directions into a seedy neighborhood, was led up stairs to a small room, and was shown a plastic wristband. Baby Finlay, it read, along with a birthdate.

Grabbing the bracelet out of his hand, Patsy put the bracelet back into a drawer. Then she demanded money, steady money to feed her habit.

My son takes a quick mouthful of Scotch, sets down his glass. "'A monthly check,' she said. She grinned at me as she rubbed her fingertips, itching for what she'd get from me."

All these years I have been not only proud but envious of my son's house, his loving marriage, his privileged children, his future. At least until the day Kathleen pointed out the crack in Brian's perfect life and wept in my kitchen. Another crack now. A big one, and this time, I feel like weeping for my own broken dream about a son. But Brian doesn't notice and keeps talking.

"I went to see her a couple of times, at her apartment, to try to convince her that the blackmail wouldn't work. By then she was prostituting and high most of the time, and I couldn't talk to her. She just held up the bracelet and smirked."

"Did she smell?" God only knows why I ask. But things are beginning to come together into some sort of pattern.

"Yeah, I guess." Distracted, he is silent for a moment. "Mostly like alcohol, cigarettes, body smells, weed sometimes. Her room was filthy, but she covered it all up with a can of orange-scented spray. Why?"

"Something...Kathleen said once. Go on." Art?

"I wanted to tell you, Mom, but you wouldn't have believed me. Or maybe you would have gone a little nuts." He's right. I'm good at going nuts. The past few months are a good example.

"So I asked Dad out for a drink, the first time I'd ever done that. When I told him about Patsy, about her blackmail. I even cried. 'I need help,' I told him. 'I can't hurt my wife, disappoint my mother.' Dad didn't say much at first, just shook his head, then he handed me one of his handkerchiefs and asked what he could do."

Brian's voice wavers. "He said that moment was the first time that he felt like he was a father."

"My God! What did he feel like for forty years if not a father?"

"Maybe unnecessary." Brian hesitates, frowns like he used to when he was ten. He's about to say something he's not sure he should. "You are a strong person, Mom. Maybe Dad couldn't find a reason to interfere with the child-raising you were doing so well. Especially since I was a surprise baby, unwanted by both of you for a time, but especially by him because..."

"Because my getting pregnant fouled up whatever dream he had held for his future life, a dream which might not have included me, as well as you." I gasp a little as I gulp the last of my Scotch. I realize that Brian's early birth has never been mentioned in our house. "How did you know?"

"I've known since I could add and subtract that I was unwanted." Brian chuckles. "I was good at math, remember?"

"Surprise, yes. Unwanted, never. You have been the center of my life, Brian. Even now, in the midst of this godawful story you are telling me. "

Would our lives have been different if this secret had not rustled below the surface of our marriage from the beginning? Probably not. Art, depressed, would have continued to be angry; I would have not forgiven him for being himself. Brian had been needed, mostly by me, as a solace to my own unhappiness.

Brian has noticed my moist eyes. He squeezes my hand, and goes on with his story. "I asked Dad to try to find my daughter, who is eighteen now. I didn't know her name, but I thought that her adoption file might now be accessible. I really wanted to know that she was happy, maybe even going to college. I thought that once I found her, knew she was all right, I could figure out how to shut Patsy up, end the blackmail. 'She's half African-American,' I told him, and he only shrugged. 'Half white,' he said. After that, Dad scribbled investment on the bottom of every check he wrote in case you found the monthly statements."

So now I know what the scraps of paper are about. As usual, Art had kept track of his expenses. "Did your father expect you to pay him back sooner or later?"

"When he got old and needed assisted living, he said. He had records, including the tab when he met with a social worker at a restaurant."

"Washington, right? And also a girl, a Latisha?"

Brian stops talking, stares at me. "How'd you know?"

"Latisha? Hair? I thought she was your father's lover."

"God, Mom." A small burst of laughter escapes him, making fun of me just like he used to when he was a teenager disbelieving the dumb thing I'd just said. "Latisha lived with the Spencers for ten years. She was taken into state custody when her father was incarcerated for big time drug dealing, and her mother had overdosed. Two foster homes later, her social worker found the Wrights, who took her in for the next six years."

"Ginnie got the two of them together, Art and Latisha?"

"She knew that Dad had the facts c
mother's name, and she'd run as check of s
She guessed that he was Latisha's father oi
didn't straighten her out on that. Since Lat
een, Ginnie asked her if she wanted to talk tc   ⌐ie who
knew her birth family. When Latisha said yes, Ginnie gave
her a phone number and when to call. The number was my
office number, and the two of them talked for a while on my
phone. Then Latisha begged Ginnie to go to dinner with her
and Art so that she could meet him. Ginnie reluctantly
agreed to join them a couple of times, then she let Latisha
make plans on her own."

"Did he ever take her to the Hilton Hotel for a night?"

"A birthday present."

"A birthday present!'

"She told him she'd never been in a hotel in her life, and
she'd really like to spend a night, order room service, look at
videos, and maybe get into the bar refrigerator. Not with
him, with the girlfriend she'd be saying goodbye to when she
had to move from the Wright's foster home. He arranged it,
paid by Visa, and said he'd never seen a grin as big as the
one she was wearing when she walked into the lobby the
next morning. With a girl. He'd been a little suspicious since
he knew she also had a boyfriend."

Brian must see the flash of anger heating my cheeks as
he describes this happy scene. He gets up, sits on the arm of
my chair, wraps an arm around my neck. "I know, Mom.
This doesn't seem like Dad, the Dad we knew. He changed.
Then on Christmas Eve..."

"Christmas Eve! Stop!" I can't listen any more. "Shit, Brian! He came in that night smelling of alcohol and cigarettes and oranges. Even half asleep I could smell him. Please don't tell me you had been with him? Boozing? And you've kept this a secret until this minute?" I get up, push Brian off my chair and walk into the bathroom. I slam the door, and I see myself in the mirror, an old woman despite my blondness, skin pale, pruny— a crazed spook, my hair standing on end, my eyes rimmed in red behind my glasses. I feel crazed, derailed, and I sit on the toilet and smell him again.

It's the whiskey breath. When one drinks only chardonnay, the whiskey smell comes through loud and clear, especially at 2 a.m. as the bed rumbles and a heavy boneless body enters it. Twice a week, sometimes, he leaves mumbling about needing some air, comes back, and his breath repels me. How dumb does he think I am? How sensory deprived? The smell lasts all night until I air out the room in the morning. His back captures the bed covers, wiping them away from me in one flail.

Brian knocks, his words garbled by the wall between us. "Mom, come on out. I need to tell you the rest of this. I need your help to know what to do next."

I open the door. "Too bad your father isn't here to help you. He apparently was a terrific helper when you asked him. I'm going to make some coffee. For both of us." Brian's grimace informs me that my words sting. Doesn't matter.

He's a grown man in a mess. What can I do? Except hope that he tells Kathleen before I feel compelled to. Five minutes later I bring two mugs of coffee out to the living room.

"Continue," I command, as the liquid sloshes on the sofa. I let Brian mop it up with a shirtsleeve.

"Dad met with Latisha pretty often, had late dinners with her after her waitress job was over. He said he could see himself in her, and her confidence was just like mine. Latisha was always up, even though she was in a tough spot. Her foster care support was ending, and her foster parents were not paid after she turned eighteen. She wanted to go college, but she'd be on her own, working full time. She wanted to be a teacher, maybe. He'd slip her a few dollars in an envelope each time they met."

"In a tan envelope?" I ask.

Brian doesn't hear me. "When Dad told me this, I borrowed ten thousand dollars from our joint account and set up a trust for Latisha, so she could plan on at least one year of college. And Dad visited Stephen Crandall and bought a life insurance policy that named Latisha and me as beneficiaries. He wanted to insure our futures, he told me. And pay me back for the college stuff. He wasn't worried about being sick or anything."

"You could have shut Patsy up by telling Kathleen about all this."

Again, the hand through the hair. "The timing was all wrong. By the time Dad found my daughter, Kathleen was in touch with a lawyer. She let me know she was unhappy with me, our life. The fact that I have an eighteen-year-old daughter would have pushed her and us over the edge. I had to clean up the mess I had created, make things right with her, with Patsy, and come to Kathleen with a clean slate, ready to start again, if she were willing."

The problem with children like my son, raised to believe they are perfect, is that they find it very difficult to admit that they are not, that they have managed to dirty the slate despite their perfect ways, and, in fact, that the slate might never come clean no matter how hard they rub. "There are no clean slates, Brian, only slates that have been erased once in a while, remnants of yesterday's chalk still clinging in the corners."

I don't say this, of course. I just pour us another inch of Scotch. We both don't talk for a while, each, I suppose, wondering where this conversation will take us.

28

Despite Brian's comment, Art had been sick. I know, because months before he died I found the container of pills,
the paper that came with it, after his last doctor's appointment. Art wouldn't talk about it. Told me it was his business, took the pills out of my hand, put them in his drawer.
That night, after he left, I found the pillbox, opened it, and
read the pills' instructions.

The pills are white, innocuous, look like aspirins. A warning
comes with them, I see when I put on my glasses and focus
on the small print. Beta blocker, the paper cautions. The
problem isn't about an overdose; it is the abrupt stopping of
the medicine, which could cause a heart to cease functioning.
I pause, fold the paper, toss it in the wastebasket.

No, I didn't dislike him enough to switch aspirins for atenolol. I'm pretty sure.

My thoughts are interrupted by a hand shaking my shoulder. "Mom? Maybe you need to rest. You look weird."

"I've been weird ever since you came in. Give me a minute, and don't talk. I need to pull myself together." I take a sip of Scotch, continue bringing it all back.

After that first thought about the aspirins, I don't go near Art's drug and vitamin drawer. I don't allow myself to remember it. Even one early morning when I scream at him about coming in smelling like a saloon, so late I believe he's left me for good.

"So, besides bourbon, what else are you doing—floozies, a sexy Viagra lover, gambling?" I try to come up with all of the possibilities. "Boys, are you into boys, like I read in the newspaper? It isn't fair to me to leave me wondering if you'll even come home. Maybe you are senile, one of those sundowner wanderers I've heard about, can't tell day from night? What?"

At that, Art grunts, which might have been the beginning of a ha.

"Just tell me." My throat hurts from shouting, and I try swallowing, but I can't. I reach for a glass of water. By now Art is sitting at the kitchen table, his hands stretched in front of him.

"You can't know yet," he says. "Maybe never, but it will be over in a while."

"I can't stand this, Art. You never talk, about anything. You have two speeds: angry and silent. I am your wife. I'd like to tell you things, but you don't listen. I would listen if you talked to me. Just..."

"Like now?" he says. His face has folded into a mask contorted by sadness. "You haven't listened for years. We've both tuned each other out. I, especially, and I've missed some good things. I took you for granted most of the time, and I missed listening to Brian. That has been the biggest loss, and there's not much I can do about it now." He shakes his head, gets up and walks like the old man he is out the back door. I don't see him for a few hours, and when he comes in, he eats a sandwich and takes a nap.

In the days following, he doesn't attempt to tell whatever he can't tell me. Then he tries one more time, on Christmas Eve. The idea of his secret festers in me like an infected splinter, and I can't listen. He dies.

Brian pours into his almost empty glass. I accept a plop in my cold coffee. "Go on," I say again. I'm finished with remembering. No turning back now.

"I saw Patsy a couple of times, tried to get her to go to another treatment center. We met at a restaurant, Boo's Soul, a place Dad told me about, because I didn't want to meet her alone, and she came in late, hair wild, on something, and told me to go fuck myself when I suggested yet another time that she needed to get clean. Her screeching caused us to be asked to leave, and I took her home. I had to carry her into her apartment, and when I came home, Kathleen didn't ask where I'd been."

Brian doesn't look at me, only into his drink. Even though I am leaning toward him, I can barely hear his words.

"I found my appointment book open on my desk. Kathleen had been looking for reasons for my being out at night. When I told him about Kathleen and the appointment book, Dad said I should stop trying to deal with Patsy, that he could take over. When I insisted that it was my problem not his, Dad said that this was the only way to save my marriage—maybe even my business, if Patsy went public, made scenes, told lies about our so-called relationship. Besides, he said, he still had some stocks. Maybe he could second-mortgage the house without you knowing."

I am stunned into silence. I can't imagine Art doing or saying any of this. "Christmas Eve?" I dare to ask.

"Mom, I'm going to try to tell about Christmas Eve just the way Dad told me. I'd never seen him like he was the night we talked about his plan to rescue me. Alive. At first, I protested, and then I finally agreed to his plan. He would go to Patsy's apartment on Christmas Eve, talk with her, take money with him and bribe her into agreeing to get back into rehab. When she moved away from here, clean, she'd receive enough money to get her resettled in a new place. Dad said that Christmas would be a new beginning for all of us."

A hollow space opens near my heart. "Did he ever mention me?"

"He said you were the best wife a man like him could have."

"And?"

"He didn't need to say any more, Mom."

I am disappointed. But what did I expect? A forty years too-late Valentine? We need to move on. "So, Christmas?"

"Dad came by our house Christmas Eve after he met with Patsy, late. Kathleen was asleep, and I'd just finished wrapping gifts, about to turn out the lights. When I invited him in, he pointed to the car and said we'd wake up everyone in the house. He was pretty drunk; he stumbled down the sidewalk, and when we got in the car, he began to talk, the words rolling out so fast I had to slow him down once in a while."

Again I can't imagine it. Words rolling out of Art.

"Dad had a couple of drinks at the Metrobar to get his courage up, and then he drove to her apartment. He found her high and babbling, and he realized she wasn't going to listen to any talk of rehab, ending the blackmail, a new life. She passed out, and as he left, he noticed her Christmas tree and what she'd hung on it." Brian held up a tiny plastic band. "He took this out of his pocket and gave it to me. 'Merry Christmas,' he said. Then Dad said something very strange. 'Even Patsy needs a tree.'"

I take the band between my fingers, read the words "Finlay girl." I have a similar band in the album I devoted to Brian's first year. "Finlay boy."

"In a tearful mush of love and alcohol, Dad described the little plastic tree. 'I didn't know a person could live such a life,' he said. Then he told me he was sorry he had failed me and added, 'We need to help her, Brian.' Somehow, he and I found each other in a whore's room, and my father had learned to love. Me. And a woman in a room that smelled of orange spray. And his granddaughter."

And maybe a woman lying awake in bed at that Christmas Eve. The best wife. That's as close as I'll ever get to touching Art's love, and maybe that's okay for now.

Brian rubs a hand over his eyes and continues. "I drove Dad home, made sure he got into the house okay and parked his car in the driveway. He said he was exhausted, hadn't slept for a week. 'Might try Patsy's pills,' he said. I told him to be careful, to not mix his meds. 'It'll be okay,' he said. 'I've forgotten to take any of my own for days.'"

29

"So Brody, now we understand, don't we?" The dog is lying beside me on the sofa, something I had forbidden when I had the strength to forbid. At the moment, I like the warmth of his body as it laps over onto mine.

Brian, relieved of a secret, has left after I advised him, like a mother is supposed to, to tell Kathleen the truth. Although perhaps painful, even destructive, this telling will lift the shroud of deceit that has wound itself around their lives. Kathleen will understand, forgive, make adjustments. Or not.

This is good advice for a guilt-ridden son. I'm not sure it works for a guilt-ridden wife. Because the man I should be talking to, listening to, touching, is dead. I had a chance to forgive, and I didn't, blinded by the smell of alcohol and orange on my husband's body.

How could I have known on Christmas Eve that the tears in Art's eyes were real?

He'd come in late but instead of creeping into bed, he sat down next to me, the dip of the mattress bringing my body next to his.

"What?" I mumbled, ready to turn away.

"I want to talk." His words slumped into each other. I could hardly hear them.

"You're drunk." I pulled at the coverlet, trying to dislocate him.

"Maybe. But that doesn't make any difference. I still have something to tell you, if you'd just listen a minute."

I remember wishing he weren't there. I heard him swear, felt him stand up. "Fuck, I feel bad about some things," he said.

"You should."

"I haven't been a very good husband. Even worse father."

His back was to me, and I pushed into my pillow and hated him for saying the words I'd wanted to hear for years, but not from a man who wouldn't remember saying them when he got up in the morning, shaky and sick to his stomach. "Go to bed."

I heard him unbutton his shirt, drop his pants to the floor. "I don't blame you," he mumbled. "You have a right to be..."

I waited for the next word, but he walked into the bathroom, closed the door. I could hear him peeing, talking to himself. To be what? Angry? Disappointed? Free of him?

I buried my head under my pillow. This last thought was too close to home.

"Are you asleep?" He had climbed into bed, was lying very still.

I pretended I didn't hear him.

"I'm a little drunk but listen. I've been doing some thinking lately. I've met someone, a young girl, who has helped me see what I've missed—"

"Shut up!" I rolled over and hit him on his shoulder with both fists. "Don't say one more word!"

"Edith."

"Not one more word!" I clutched the headboard as I pulled myself away. "Don't ever talk to me again! Talk to your new girlfriend. Drink with her. Do whatever you want with her, but do not talk to me!" I covered my head again, and I suppose I slept. In the light of day, that midnight scene seemed like a bad dream and it slipped away as dreams do when one wakes up and faces the morning and a Christmas brunch and a dead husband.

I must be crying because Brody is even closer, leaning into me. I wrap an arm around him, wipe a cheek on the top of his head, and then give in to the grief flooding me. We stay there, not moving, for a long time.

The next morning, maybe to lessen my guilt, maybe just to talk again to a girl Art had somehow learned to love, I call Latisha at her new apartment. A cheery voice answers on the first ring, tells me she is Kimberly and that Latisha won't be home until about dinnertime. "She's with her father," Kimberly adds. "Left about an hour ago. Do you want to leave a message?"

I must sound like a safe old lady for her to offer that information. Or maybe Kimberly needs a class in telephone discretion, along with whatever else she is enrolled in. And I'm confused by the mention of a father, and I can't come up with a message, except that I'm Edith, and I'll try again later. I add, "She's with Mr. Wright, right?" I don't know how I remembered her foster father's name.

"I didn't catch his name. And I'll tell her. Bye." And Kimberly is off, and I am left holding a dead phone. Now what? I spend the rest of the day taping up paint chips on the walls of the dining room and pretending to make decisions. Then I turn on the TV and let the tube make decisions for me.

"You and Brody want to go for a walk?" Kathleen is at the door, smiling, and I grab the leash, a jacket, and we three head out in the late afternoon sun, down the sidewalk heading for the river. I find it difficult to look at her. I know too much.

"Great day!" my daughter-in-law says. "How have you been? You look a little peaked. Eating okay?" She's full of pep, walking briskly and I have to take long steps to keep up with her. Brody slows us down at every tree, allowing me to catch my breath once in a while.

"I'm fine. You seem perky. What's happening?" I'm quite sure her news, whatever it is, will not be the news I'm keeping locked inside, hoping it won't leak out in some thoughtless moment. Not my business, I tell myself—unless Brian has confessed to her as he did to me last night. Listening to her soft laughter at one of Brody's p-mail stops, I can guess he did not.

"Mom, I finally feel as if I have some control over my life. I've talked with a divorce lawyer, and on his advice, I'm going to ask Brian to move out. We can do this in a civilized way, the kids being the center of any negotiations, and they need to stay in their house, go to their school, have the same friends. Brian can go ahead with whatever or whomever he is involved without worrying about the children or me, and I am going to go back to work. I've already interviewed at a tech company." She's talking fast, smiling a little at that last comment as if she can see a new life ahead of her.

"And what does Brian say?"

"I haven't told him yet. I wanted to be sure before I made any decisions. After the weekend you took care of the kids when I pleaded with him to tell me what was going on, and he didn't, I realized that we were already separated, had been maybe for months. Then I found out about the $15,000 gone from our savings and that did it. I don't do well when I've lost control of what should be my life."

I can't help saying it. "Maybe Brian has lost control, too."

"Or not. Maybe he's taking control of some part of his life I have no part in. So I'm freeing him to keep it up without a wife to fuck things up."

Kathleen must believe that the word will make her brave enough to pull off this plan. Maybe it's a symbol of her renewing self: strong, independent, not to be messed with by anyone. Including me. Although I'd like to grab her shoulders and shake her, I won't. I will not tell her the truth, as much as I know it, about Brian. That's his job. Once again, I hope my son is up to it. Why do I keep doubting his courage? Perhaps because I, myself, have so little of it. I've never faced up to anyone, to Art, without recoiling, sinking back into bitchy submission.

I stumble over a curb, and Kathleen takes my arm. "Careful, bifocals are dangerous." It isn't the bifocals that make me stumble; it is the realization that Art hadn't turned away those last months. He had stepped right into the thick of Brian's life and stayed there until the moment he died. When he tried to talk to me about what was happening to him, I shouted at him to shut up.

I stop, wait with Brody a moment, then I tell Kathleen I need to go home. "I know you are making difficult decisions right now, Kathleen. You need to talk to Brian tonight, to make sure you are listening to each other." Brody and I turn back toward home. "I wish I had listened," I call over my shoulder.

Kathleen just keeps walking, a little faster now.

30

I know I have it somewhere, that poem I wrote on that napkin. What was I wearing that night? I check the pockets of
my coats hanging in the closet, pull out odd bits and pieces
and have just about given up when I feel a wad in the bottom of my red jacket pocket. I pour a cup of coffee and sit
down at my kitchen table and remember that day I met
Seth. If I'm careful as I smooth out the napkin, I will be able
to reconstruct the words, remember a little more, perhaps.
Ah, here it is: In this foreign place I may uncover a clue to a
mystery I never felt, did not grasp, some scrap of truth that
will lead me to a man I never met."

Damn! The man I never met is being introduced to me
by our son, and indeed a scrap of truth is floating up to the
surface. To my surface, at least. Yesterday's walk with

Kathleen told me that she also has a man she's never met, or has forgotten she's met him in the rush of life, truth fluttering just out of her reach.

For now, I'll try to decide what to do about Seth, whom I walked out on at that restaurant table.

Strange how truth makes a person do something she's going to regret. I would like to apologize for my bad behavior, to explain how deceived I felt when I knew he had more truth than I did. Now my pot of truth is flowing over, and I'm astonished by it and no longer angry. I'm, what is the word? Anticipatory, like the moment just before Art and I married, and I had my whole life ahead of me. No, that's not a good example. I was scared. For good reason.

I have to stop meandering in the past, both my own and my son's. I need to go forward, to maybe next week. I will apologize to Seth, tell him I'm sorry for leaving him with two full plates and no one to talk to, ask him to come here, to my home. I am anticipatory. My fingers shake as I page through the telephone book, look for Boo's Soul, punch the numbers, ask for Seth Benjamin.

"Sorry, Seth is not here today. Can I take a message?"

"MiKaela, is that you? This is Edith, looking for Art, except I'm not looking for him anymore, and I'd love to talk to Seth." I'm babbling like a high school girl.

"Of course, Edith. Seth said he'd had dinner with you. Did he tell you what he was celebrating that night? He's at his new restaurant, Magnolia, downtown. He'll be there until all the bugs get worked out with the serve staff. I'll be going over next week as maitresse d' or whatever they call it. Come see us!"

"Magnolia? Does it have a phone?" Stupid. High school again.

MiKaela doesn't seem to notice. "Sure! He'd love to show you the new place!"

I write down the telephone number, the pencil wobbling across the notepad, and I hang up and then without pausing, I dial. If I had even taken a deep breath, I would not have dared.

His voice, low, masculine, murmurs, "Magnolia," and I squeak, "Edith."

He laughs his growly laugh and tells me to come by. He'll save me a table at six o'clock in the window. Then he laughs again. "I need you to attract classy ladies to come in."

He gives me the address and adds, "I'm glad you called." After we hang up, I go to my closet and wonder what I should wear. Being downtown, Magnolia is probably a little dressier than Boos, maybe even the Hilton. I call Lynne.

"You're going to Magnolia? It's gotten rave reviews in the Oregonian. I'm so impressed!"

Lynne doesn't know the half of it. I'll explain everything soon, but right now I want to know what to wear.

"Black pants, silk blouse, something bright over your shoulders, and don't worry about shoes, except no Nikes. Short heels. Everyone is going bare-legged these days."

"Not me."

"Okay, knee nylons. And get a blow dryer for your newly blond hair. Drip dry only works on eighteen-year-olds. Little purse over your shoulder to hold lipstick and cab fare home if it doesn't go well."

"What do you mean, if it doesn't go well?"

"It didn't go so well last time, did it? So plan ahead and be ready for anything."

"Anything?" Now I'm even more worried.

"Breath mints."

"Oh."

"And maybe..."

"What?"

"That's for next time. Just go with the flow, and we'll talk more tomorrow. I'm proud of you, friend." She covers the mouthpiece. It's Wednesday. "In a minute, honey, this is important."

I don't like to drive downtown, and I call Information and find out that Magnolia is on the bus line in the center of the city. I slide one dollar in the toll box and realize I'm the only one on the bus not in athletic shoes. I tuck my two-inch heels under me and hope I know where to get off. A purple-haired young man sits next to me.

"Tourist?" he asks.

"No, I live here. Where are you from?"

"Right now, here, but I've been in California for a while. Way too hot down there. This town's cool. In lots of ways."

"Like?"

"Music, lots of local art. I'm in tech. Me and my partner just got venture capital to work on a new invention."

"Venture capital?" What language are we talking here?

"Yeah, we've a plan that will let people like you get on
public transportation without a ticket, just a magnetic strip
on your credit card. Save a lot of time and maybe make
money for the city. Oops, here's where I get off." The young
man moves to the door and glances back at me. "Remember
you knew me when..."

Damn. Who couldn't like an attitude like that for a
change? I'm feeling a little optimistic myself. I need to get
off at the next stop, and I walk the block and a half to the
restaurant. Seth is waiting for me at the door.

Magnolia is low-lit and flowing with soft, indeterminate
music. A wooden bar lines one wall, and a long upholstered
bench and small tables line the other; placemats and napkins
are laid out on each. Larger tables covered with green cloths
are scattered in the space between the walls, and every table, even the small ones, holds a pint-sized canning jar filled
with blue and yellow wildflowers. Candles flicker under the
flowers, making them glow in the soft light. At the few oc-
cupied tables, old milk bottles hold water, the water glasses
the squatty barrels I remember from my mother's cup-
boards.

Seth leads me to a small table near the window, and as I
slide behind it on the bench, I feel the soft brush of mohair.
"Like my grandma's sofa," I say. I'm taken back sixty years.
"The whole place feels like grandma."

Seth grins. "Just what I wanted. My grandma, too. Wait
until you see the menu. Magnolia is down home. Like we
remember it when we were kids. Most everything slow
cooked, roast chicken and dumplings, pot roast, homemade

sauerkraut and pig knuckles, vegetable soup simmering on the back of the stove, apple and rhubarb pie just out of the oven."

"Liver and onions, mashed potatoes?"

"Certainly. The only up-to-date items on the menu are the wines. Our bar is prepared to make any drink you crave from way back then, including one my father called "hootch," fermented from unsold potatoes from the farm, which a local distillery has modified to produce a similar, but better tasting, product."

I'm sent for a moment into a back seat of a Plymouth, two young people reeling from desire and homemade gin, going at it. I blink the memory away.

Seth sits across the table from me. His remarkable eyes take me in, slowly. I can hardly hear what he's saying, but I can tell from the ring of his words that he is joyful. How long has it been since I've used that word to describe someone? And his joy is spilling over into me, filling me up until I say, "I'm so glad I know you."

I haven't planned to say that. It just comes out. And it is true. But I am embarrassed, and I add, "And to be invited to your wonderful restaurant."

Seth's suddenly solemn. He leans toward me, says, "And I'm very glad to know you, handsome lady." Then he signals to the waiter lingering behind us. "We're ready, Jeff. White wine, and then we'll order." I'm glad he hasn't ordered hootch. I have a feeling it would be even worse than red wine, headache-wise, middle-of-the-night-bad-memory-wise.

Magnolia fills up by seven o'clock, and Seth excuses himself to greet people at their tables. When he comes back, I've finished my liver and onions (my mother never doused hers with wine, I'm pretty sure...a pity) and I thank him and leave as the second seating is arriving. He's busy. That's good. I'll get out of the way, and as I leave, he tells me he'll call me in the morning. This time I believe that promise.

31

And he does.

"I left you stranded last night. We didn't have time to talk about whatever upset you the last time we sat down to dinner, and I'm pretty sure it wasn't the creamed mushrooms. I hope you're feeling better about things."

I'm glad that he leaves the things part unstated. He must know that my dead husband, my son, and Latisha have all landed onto my daily list of things to obsess over. He's sensitive enough to let me do the talking if I want to. I do. But not over the phone. "I'm understanding it all a little better, but it's not over yet. After I walked out of the Hilton, I must have left you with the impression that I was angry at you. Isn't there a saying about killing the messenger? That's why I called you yesterday."

"To check to see if I'm dead?"

"To apologize. Hearing the truth is hard sometimes. I'm not good at it. But I'm learning. I know you're busy, Seth, but I'd love to talk to you sometime soon. Here, at my house, lunch, glass of wine? Next week?" I'm not sure why I put our meeting off almost a week from now. Maybe I hope that everything will be okay by then.

So we agree on breakfast on Monday, the day Magnolia is closed. I'll cook, and we'll talk, and who knows what else?

I don't hear from Lynne after Brody and I have walked, and I do the wash, which is a lot smaller now that there is only one of us. I still fold the clothes on the bed, watching Perry Mason, but my hands miss folding the seven or eight tee-shirts I used to get so riled up about and the jockey underwear, bleached white, the holey ones tossed away every so often. Perry is only half finished and I'm done when the phone rings.

"So, how was it? The food, the little purse with supplies, the good-looking man? Tell me everything."

I don't want to disappoint Lynne. "It was pleasant," I answer. "I left at about seven when the crowd started arriving. He is a nice man."

"And?"

"And nothing. Except that he'll come for breakfast next week." I try to change the subject. I don't want to let the anticipation that has lingered behind the scenes since his call evaporate in small talk. "Is your Wednesday/Saturday man gone? Finally? Now what?"

"Breakfast? A good, subtle move. And yes, he's gone, and I'm about to clean the house. Life goes on, even after the Wednesday/Saturday man. Our routine is a little like being married, you know? Boring at times. Only he leaves instead of lying about in his lounger for days. Which reminds me. What is happening with your search for Art and the mysterious young lady?"

I don't like the joking tone of Lynne's question. "Not funny, friend."

"Sorry. I guess I'm a little upset about being out of the loop. We haven't talked for a while. I'll start again. How are you?"

"You're right, it's an exclusive loop, three persons: me, Art and Brian. Out of the loop, Kathleen is asking for a divorce. Brian has chosen to hide a secret, two secrets, about his father and about himself and the 'mysterious young lady,' as you called her. Latisha, who is a relative of some sort to me."

"Kidding!'

"I can't tell you even though I know you are the best person to talk to because I'm waiting for Brian to do what he needs to do." Again, I'm holding back from my friend, because of the silent dread that lurks behind each word.

"I promise that you and I will share several glasses of wine and the whole story when the time is right."

"And I'm worrying about being bored with my Wednesday/Saturday man." I know Lynne is raising her eyebrows. "I love you, friend. Be strong. This is just another Mt. Hood, only not so cold. I'll wait for your call and the chardonnay."

⟨✍⟩

"We've come to walk Brody and maybe have mac and cheese." Kathleen stands behind Meg and Winston and mouths, "Okay?"

"Sure, we need some company here." I reach for the screen door knob as Kathleen says, "I'll be back early this evening." She turns away so quickly I don't have time to do anything but open the door wider and let the kids in. "So, besides surprising your grandma, what have you been up to?"

Both children go silent for a moment, then Meg says, her lips quivering, "We helped Daddy pack. He's going away for a while."

Winston gives her a knock on the shoulder. "Shut up. Mom said not to say." His brows lower as he glares at her. Then he recovers. "Dad is going on a little trip. He'll be back soon." I can't stand the lie wriggling under his words.

"Well, I'm just glad you are here. I've been a little lonesome lately, me and Brody. He needs some energetic walking and ball tossing. Maybe I do, too." I throw on the sweater that hangs on a hook in the hall and open the door. "Let's go. It'll do us all some good."

It's all I can do to keep up. Poor Brody. He has to put up with walking with an old lady when I'm sure that he prefers running with two much younger leash holders. "Wait at the corner!" I call, not for safety as much as for me to catch my breath. "Let's go to the dog park. You guys can run there, and I can watch." The dog park also has an umbrella and a bench for doddering owners like me.

The kids find a ball, mangy-looking, left behind by a careless dog or owner, and they throw it again and again, and Brody brings it back like an obedient four-legged yoyo. They want me to throw it, but the ball is mushy with dog saliva, and while I don't mind a thin layer on my ankles, I don't like a cup of it in my hand. "You do it."

The three of them finally are finished with the game, the children pushing their hot bodies next to me on the bench, and the dog allowing his long red tongue to ventilate him. We are quiet for a while, watching a huge, hairy, black mastiff gallop into a cluster of Labradoodles and scatter them in all directions. A dog that big would take over the house, the sofa, and the kitchen, and the bed. I look at Brody and know he's the right size for me. He lowers his head and licks my ankle.

"Grandma?"

This title is again precious and two earnest faces turn my way, not smiling, needing something from me. "Yep."

"Why is Daddy going away?" Even her brother's elbow does not stop her. "I don't want him go anywhere."

My answer comes easily, like a lie. "Sometimes parents have to go places, Meg. They return after a while. You'll see." Am I lying? Yes. "Your daddy loves you so much, both of you. He told me so many times." This is lying, but it also is the truth. "So, he doesn't want you to worry. He wants you to keep your mother company because she probably will miss him, too." Damn. Why lay that on them? These children have no responsibility in the disaster their parents are creating. "What they really want is for each of you to..."

What? Be unaffected by what is happening to their families? To deny that something is indeed changing drastically in their lives? No.

"What they really want you to do is to ask them the question you just asked me. Because they love you, they will tell you the truth." I touch a cheek ready for a tear, pat a head as it drops toward a chest. Time to change the subject. I breathe, make my voice perky. "Grandmas know a lot, but they don't know everything. We do know how to make mac and cheese and to find Princess Bride on the TV, which I suggest we do as soon as we get home. But let's walk a little slower this time, okay?"

I am exhausted not by the idea of walking back home but by the cheery positivity I've forced, like a magician, out of the foreboding chill that has filled me.

Kathleen, tearless and unsmiling, picks up her children's coats "He's moved out," she whispers. The children are asleep on the sofa. Princess Bride has wiped them out. She sorts sleeves and pushes her children's limp arms into them.

"It's going to be okay, Edith," she says as she walks them, their eyes wanting to close as they stumble, to the car. Kathleen looks back, adds, "Really, Mom." and I don't believe her. Or Brian, who has tried to assure me with the same words. Nothing will be okay for a long time, maybe ever, unless my son screws his courage to the sticking point and tells his wife the truth. Where did that phrase come from? Sophomore English, the Shakespearean quote that spoke to a timid, uncertain girl who didn't have a clue what courage was, but who knew she could use some.

So can Brian, child of my upbringing and my genes. It is time to make an adjustment, if not in genetic correction, in my parenting. A forty-seven-year-old son is still a son, may need a surge of upbringing even now. In the morning, I call Kathleen to find out where he is.

Kathleen doesn't answer her phone. This may take a little longer than I expect.

32

In the meantime, I don't have to call Latisha again. She calls me. Did I describe myself as anticipatory once? This girl is definitely in that category.

"I'm going to meet my birth mother."

"Is that good?" I must sound shocked.

"I've always wanted to. And now someone has called me and told me that he can help me find her."

"What kind of someone?" Couldn't be Brian. He doesn't work that way, offering unexpected gifts. He'd...what would he do? "Did he ask for money?"

"Only his expenses. Maybe $500 he said. He has friends in the Children's Services Division, and they are willing to search through closed files for a few hundred dollars and find out information that will help him find her. I really want to do this, to know, you know? About me? I don't want my parents to be a mystery any longer. I don't care what she turns out to be like, I just want to know."

So Brian hasn't told Latisha. The father she'd gone out with a few days ago was a different father, Mr. Wright, maybe. And I'm assuming since I haven't heard from her, Brian hasn't talked to Kathleen. It's been four days since he confessed to me. What's he waiting for? Does he hope that I'll do the dirty work? I consider it. Absolutely not. My son needs to face his truth, his wife, and his daughter. I have no part in this. Except, perhaps, to remind him of his responsibility, like a mother would. To take him by the ear and scream into it. I tell Latisha to wait a day or two. I call Brian's office.

I hope to be calm, supportive, mature, but when I open my mouth the words spew out, hot, uncontrollable. "Brian, Latisha is about to pay some sleazeball to find her mother, her drug-crazed, sick, whore of a mother. For God's sake, wouldn't a thoughtful, penitent, only slightly-deranged father be better to find? What in the hell are you waiting for?" I would have gone on raving, but Brian orders me to stop, to catch my breath. So I do and I can hear him breathing a little himself.

"Okay," he finally says. "I'm coming by. For lunch. Fried egg sandwich, please. Over easy."

I try to calm myself by recalling past egg sandwiches. They go back a long way. He used to like them juicy, the yolk runny and dripping down his chin. Mayonnaise. He'll have to deal with the whole wheat bread that has replaced the white fluff I used to buy.

Strange how food rules change over the years. As I take out the egg carton, my thoughts drift in a distractive swarm. Wonder Bread was expensive compared to the local brands, but I wanted the best for my child. I bought butter instead of margarine and Crisco instead of lard. To help him grow, we ate red meat at almost every dinner, along with potatoes and gravy and always a dessert, cake or pie. Then after Brian moved out and I started buying pants with elastic waists, a slew of diet books came out promising healthy hearts and low body fat ratios. Sounded good to me. I haven't cooked red meat for years, except in a stew or two. For a year, I quit eating eggs, but gave in about the same time I also discovered that olive oil was okay. Art grumbled at my weekly stir fry, but I now understand that in that last year, he got his starches elsewhere, maybe at Boo's Soul.

Sometimes it seems as if there are no old rules anymore, only new ones, like the no-sugar, eat-greens, drink-gallons-of-water that Kathleen runs her kitchen by, and the rules change with every new scientific study. Everyone is looking for some kind of certainty in life. The only certainty that I can detect at this point is that there is no certainty. One, maybe—that one will never know when she will wake up dead. Or he.

When I say that out loud to Brody, he puts his head on my thigh and nudges me. Perhaps he's telling me that he doesn't want to hear any more dismalness. Or, more likely, he's reminding me that I have butter close to burning on the stove. I return to the task at hand, crack the eggs into the pan.

I'm flipping the fried egg onto the mayonnaised bread when Brian knocks and comes in. I've pulled myself together and I say, "Here you go," as I hand him his sandwich and glass of skim milk. That's another thing, I almost say out loud. Blue non-fat milk. But instead, I pour myself a cup of coffee, good for me, according to the latest report, and sit down at the table, my mouth shut.

Brian ummms once or twice, takes a huge bite and washes it down with the milk, just like he used to. Some things don't change. Like the boy-innocent look he gives me as he pushes the empty plate away.

"So this is what is happening, Mom. When Dad and I talked that last night, one of the last things he said was that he didn't know how a person like Patsy could live such a life. 'We need to help her,' he said. I thought about that after he died. By then, I thought I'd done everything I could do, including paying for rehab, and I got repaid by her trying to blackmail me. I wanted to forget her, to get back to living the life I was supposed to have. I tried to, coming home on time, getting involved with the kids, with Kathleen." Brian shrugs, finishes his milk.

"It worked for a few weeks. Then I started worrying about another child of mine, a girl Dad really cared about. We'd worked out the college money stuff, and our attorney took over the trust management. But the whole situation didn't feel right. Dad's words, the 'we' part, kept coming back, making me feel even more guilty."

"Too many secrets can curdle a plan," I suggest. "You said you would be talking to Kathleen. Have you?"

Brian looks over my shoulder, as if the answer is somewhere behind me. "It might be too late." After a moment, he manages to meet my eyes. "Kathleen asked me to move out, to take time to evaluate what we are doing and what we want, and I have. She seems so sure, so ready to move away from our marriage. I couldn't tell her about Patsy and Latisha because especially now, with the mess almost all cleaned up, that information would push her away even faster." Brody lays his chin on Brian's knee and gazes up at him. Brian's thumb gently brushes the dog's forehead, as he continues: "I can't imagine not being married to Kathleen."

No, I don't suppose he can. "It still unfinished, the cleaning up of the slate?"

Brian gets up, finds a glass and Art's Scotch, liquid still sloshing at the bottom. He pulls out a handful of ice cubes, drops them in the liquor, looks up and asks, "This all right?"

He's still my son, looking for permission. "Sit down and keep talking." I sound a little like Art.

He sits, raises his glass to his lips, for courage, maybe. "Dad had said, in that unsmiling, serious way of his, that we needed to take care of Patsy. So I went back to see her a few times, trying to understand how I could do that. She accused me of killing her, that I needed to give her money before she ended up dead in a gutter. One night she promised that that she could try harder to get clean if she didn't have to whore and live around the druggies who squatted on her street."

"Shit," I said. "Blackmail again."

Shaking his head, he disagrees. "I realized she was right. She had to leave that hole of an apartment and get back into a recovery situation. The first rehab didn't work. She was there for thirty days, sure she was cured, then two days later she was right back where she'd started. I had to find a different place for her, and I had to be ready to pay for it."

"The fifteen thousand dollars."

"Right. The Avalon program lasts three months, longer if necessary, at a country estate where the clients understand they cannot leave early without the permission of the doctors who run the place. If they do, they lose their money and the possibility of ever returning. I described the program, told her I might be able to find her a job when it was all over, and then I drove her to the clinic. She listened to the director, walked through the rooms, met a couple of clients, and agreed she would do it. When I asked her why, she started crying. She said that when I first came to her door, she saw only money, then later she began to see that she might have a chance, not only to get clean but maybe to meet her daughter. 'I won't fuck this one up,' she promised. She wiped her nose and pointed a finger at me. 'And you keep watch over our girl until I'm ready to invite her into my life. Maybe she'll invite me into hers, too.'"

"She knew about Latisha? What had happened to her?"

"I had told her that my father had been looking for Latisha, had found her, that she was a beautiful young woman. That she would be proud of her."

"So, why the secrecy? Latisha wants to meet her birth mother, and her birth mother wants to meet her." I eye the bottle, decide on iced tea.

"Seemed right to wait for Patsy to get on her feet. Then last month she had a relapse. I'm not sure how it works, but something about the body fighting to not give up the chemicals it's gotten used to. She had to be sedated, confined and continue to go through withdrawal, painful as it was. She's doing better now. She's allowed to leave the clinic for an hour or two with an approved friend. The doctor says it will be a while before she'll feel strong enough to go into a halfway house, and after that, she can begin her life again." Brian drains his glass, sets it in the sink, looks out into the yard as if he can detect the next place. "She wants to go to college with her daughter."

Now I do need a drink. I can see the next place: a tall beautiful girl and her scummy mother walking down a campus sidewalk talking about their psychology class, both of them supported with money from the troubled, uncertain man standing at my window. And a grandfather, a gentling ghost.

I gather my motherhood up. "First things first. And the first thing is your marriage." I can remember getting riled up like this when he was ten and needed to straighten up and fly right. I move in close to him. "You have a couple of things to take care of before anything good can happen. You know what they are. While Patsy is in treatment, you need to introduce Latisha to her father and to her half brother and sister and her stepmother." I pause, squeeze his arm, hard. "And before you do that, you have to tell Kathleen everything you have told me, letting the chips fall where they may."

My grandfather chopped down trees for the firewood that heated the old house. One day I followed him into the woods and watched as he hacked at a trunk. Bits of wood flew out at each axe stroke until the ground was covered with white chips, the tree down and ready to be sawed into stove lengths. Grandpa saw me collecting the white bits in my coat pockets and said, "They're too wet. Let the chips fall where they may." Not his own original thought, of course, but the next year I found that the little pieces of alder had melted into the soil, gone except for a stump nearby waiting to be dragged out by an old tractor.

"Telling the truth is kind of like chopping at a stubborn tree, pieces of what-was dropping to the earth and disappearing," I say.

I hand my son an axe—the words I love and I trust you—as he opens the door.

He looks back, and then he shuffles away like an old man, as old as his dead father. He shakes his head. And I understand that while I love him, will continue to love him, trust no longer exists. Perhaps he knows this, knows my axe is dull.

33

As Brian drives away, my knees go weak, and I wonder if I am going to pass out. Brody follows me to the lounger, and I sink into it and try to decide if I'm having an attack of some sort. No pain in my arm, I can wiggle my feet, my eyes are blurry, but they usually are. I ask Brody, "Wow, dog, what's going on?" so I'm able to speak. But my hands, legs, most of the rest of me are trembling as if something inside is trying to break through my skin. I rest my head against the chair. I have felt this way once before. When?

Then I remember. I was seventeen, and my mother had just pulled my hair and called me a loose chippy and had locked my bedroom door as she left. She had seen Art's and my entangled arms and legs flailing in back seat of the car he'd parked next to the neighbor's hedge. She'd been waiting for us, hiding behind a hydrangea bush.

"You spied on us!"

"And I'll keep doing it. You can't go on embarrassing us in front of the neighbors like this. We're good Christian people, and so is everyone else around here, except a certain mouthy young woman with no thought for anyone else but herself. Shape up or ship out, girl."

After she left I curled up under my quilt and tried to quiet the surge of anger that was making my legs twitch and my lungs close up. I told myself, "I'm okay, I'm okay," even though I was pretty sure I was not, on several fronts. I didn't feel very innocent about what we'd been doing, not only that night, but for quite a few nights. And it would be embarrassing if Mr. Jeffrey came out and knocked on the window and asked us to leave. And I couldn't imagine facing my father over the breakfast table in the morning. He still believed I was his little girl.

No, I wasn't okay. But it isn't fair to spy on a person, was it? Another wave of anger at my mother sent my skin tingling.

When I finally stopped moaning into my pillow, I began to reinterpret the message she gave to me before she slammed the door. If I heard her right, Art and I could do anything we wanted as long as she and the neighbors didn't know. That meant Dad, too. I felt better. Not so guilty, still angry, but the jerking legs calmed down. I raised my head from my pillow and filled my lungs with the cool air flowing from under the raised sash at the foot of my bed.

And Art and I continued to make out in his car, only not anywhere near the Jeffrey hedge, and only a swelling stomach months later forced me to ship out and start my next life with my lover.

Anger is making me tremble like that girl I once was. Anger at my son. Anger, mixed with guilt, just like before. Somehow, I have managed to raise a coward. I'm responsible for a man destroying not only his own life but the lives of his family. Brian believes that the truth will cause more pain than his disappearance. After my arm-squeezing, metaphor of a lecture, he didn't say a word. He just turned towards the door.

When did I teach him that running away solved anything? Perhaps every time I couldn't find the courage to deal with the truth of my marriage, the many moments I walked away from the words and bruises that had crushed any hope of love. I couldn't disrupt the childhood of my son; and I couldn't face becoming the hapless woman who had no skills to keep herself alive. So, afraid, I didn't try to change Art's and my unspoken contract. He worked, came home, ate and criticized. I kept a house, raised a cautious son, allowed the boy's love to fill my empty places.

I am now experiencing the results of burying myself behind narrowed eyes and grudgingly-offered meals and in the left-hand side of a cold bed. The painful words that burst from Art's lips, his dark thoughts, were fed by my bitterness. Brian, handicapped by overweening mother-love, grew up in a home devoid of normal love. And now he's about to create a home just like it. My fault.

I pour a glass of wine, overwhelmed with regret.

The phone rings. I break out of the fog that envelopes me and answer it. It's Latisha, in the lunchroom at school, I can tell by the din of voices competing for mine. She seems happy to talk to me and happy in general. "What's up with you?" she asks, giggling at something someone has said. "Oh, I have something to tell you."

"Yeah?" I'm not going to like what comes next, I'm sure.

"Yeah. That guy you know I told you about? Well, I looked him up and found out he's just been released from jail, and he's waiting for a trial for lying to people. Fraud, they call it. Guess I was lucky, wasn't I, not to fall for his scam?"

She's apparently sipping through a straw, at the bottom of whatever she's drinking. A sloshy gurgle erupts. And then, "I still want to find her, you know. Should I go to the agency and ask Ginnie?"

"Sounds like a good idea." What am I saying? Somewhere in my mother's heart I want Brian to do this, despite the slight chance that he will, and I need to give him a few days' time to grow up. "Why don't I go with you? I'm busy until next Monday or so, but I'd love to sit in on the conversation with the social worker. Give you a little support, maybe?"

Latisha is consulting a calendar of some sort. "I have two classes on Monday, but I am free after three. It's close to the

Lincoln building. I could walk over. Should I make an appointment with Ginnie?"

"I'll do it. If she has the time, I'll get back to you." I try to sound as carefree as the blossoms of glee bursting behind my granddaughter, an attitude I might enjoy if I can ever laugh again. When I call, Ginnie seems delighted that Latisha and I will be coming by her office. "She wants to know about her birth mother," I add. "I'd like to sit in on the conversation, maybe give her a little support."

"Three o'clock," she confirms. "See you Monday."

Brody is frowning at me. Have I forgotten to feed him? Yes. I pour out his kibbles and pour myself another glass of wine. I wait for this day to be over.

34

Shit. Could I have been more vague, more timid? Chips? He'll not decide because of anything I've said. I've always been too fearful to be convincing. I should have slapped him, threatened that if he didn't get this mess straightened out immediately that I would do it myself. I should have talked to him like I talked to his father. Been the shrew I've been working on for years. Maybe then his anger at me would have given him the guts to tell the truth to his wife. Now that would have been a sharp axe!

Stop. I can't go on babbling these thoughts. Nothing I do will strengthen the backbone of the depressed man who walked away from my door an hour ago. Maybe nothing I do will.

I escape into a nap.

An hour later, my eyes spring open, startled awake by the realization that I have a breakfast date with Seth, here, Monday morning. I'd almost forgotten. How easily I forget the good things lately. I get out my notepad. It's a relief to have something other than my son to obsess about.

I'm glad I've worked on the house. It no longer resembles a museum of 1970's knickknacks. I need fresh flowers, though, and maybe one of those new coffeepots that make lattes and espresso. And cups for the lattes, large, round bowls with saucers, and...I make a list. This casual brunch will cost me a couple hundred dollars, I realize, as the list moves onto the second page. So what? I've always wanted to have cappuccinos on demand, haven't I? Actually, no, but I didn't know I wanted blond hair, either. Or fewer valleys at the ends of my lips. Can't do anything about that before Monday, except maybe visit Phoenix for a make-over at her cosmetics counter. I call her, and she can take me later this afternoon.

"I'll be back, Brody," I reassure him. "After I've filled a few hours of not thinking about what I'm really thinking about." Brody looks at me as if I'm out of my mind, and I agree with him.

When I get back it is nearly dinnertime, and the dog needs to go out. We don't walk, because I don't want to spoil my face. As I warm up some soup, I wonder if I'll have to sleep sitting up for the next three nights for the same reason. I look pretty good for an old lady, a handsome old lady, I correct myself. I'm glad I took notes and bought more product after Phoenix worked on me. But I'm not washing this off until I have to.

I do what I've been avoiding doing ever since I walked in the door. I look at the phone. No message light is flashing. I pick it up, just in case. The usual buzz. But, I tell myself, if Brian and Kathleen are in the midst of a marriage-shaking conversation, why would either of them call me?

Tomorrow, I'll hear, I tell myself, as I pick up the Oregonian and take the Arts and Entertainment section to bed with me.

Instead, in the middle of the night I hear from someone else as I drift through a flood of guilt and sadness that fills my heart, leaving me floating aimless on a black silent sea. I stir as a ghost of a scent, orange citrus, alcohol wafts by.

I feel Art's breath on my neck. His hand touches my shoulder and moves downward until his fingers reach my breast. Tiny waves of pleasure flow from my nipple, and my breathing slows and I'm afraid to disrupt the rhythm echoing through other parts of my body.

"I'm sorry," I hear him say.

I don't want to open my eyes. But I do. The room is dark. I am alone and my breath comes in soft gasps. I lower my eyelids and wish him back.

He is gone, but I want to tell him that I am sorry, too. I say it out loud, and I wonder if he can hear me as clearly as I heard him.

Perhaps it doesn't matter.

Will I ever reveal this dream to anyone, Art's last words to me, my words to him? Probably not. This is between my husband and myself. I go to sleep.

I did not take the makeup off last night. My pillow is a modern piece of art, pink, black streaks, purple smudges. I'm tempted to frame it, as a remembrance of a midnight meeting, a dispelling of regret and guilt, for both of us, maybe. Brody twitches anxiously as I swing my legs over the side of the bed and stand up. Unbelievably, the clock says it's ten o'clock. The sleep of the innocent, or at least a forgiven and forgiving soul .

"Let's go, dog," I call to him as he paws anxiously at the door. I pull my pants on, tuck my hair under a cap. I don't look at myself in the mirror. Another modern piece of art, I suspect, which I'll have to explain to anyone I meet on the sidewalk, including the mailman who is standing on my porch, a pile of catalogues in his hands. "I'm waiting for the million-dollar check which will come any day," I say, averting my face.

"Hope springs eternal," Bob answers. "But you do have an official-looking letter here. Maybe it's what you are waiting for?" He looks at me and grins. "Big night?"

"Senior moment involving new make-up," I say. The letter in his hand has a return address of California Mutual Insurance. I take it and the rest of the junk mail and set it on the table next to the door. "Brody says 'hurry' so we're off." I leave Bob continuing to sort from his wheeled cart, and the dog and I rush down the sidewalk to the empty lot, our emergency potty. I could use one myself, but Brody needs to walk a little after a day of lying around in the house, so we move on to the dog park. I sit on the bench, and he joins the romping mass of friends in the center of the lawn. I am not romping in any sort of way. Instead, I am close to mindlessness; an unusual peace has settled in, and I hope it's permanent.

When he's had enough, the dog nudges my knee and lets me know it's time to eat. We head home.

The kibble is rattling in the dog dish, and I've used the toilet and washed my face when I remember the official-looking envelope. I risk a paper cut and slip my nail under the flap. My sense of peace is dissipating. This could mean thousands of dollars lost to Brian and Latisha and indeed, a re-igniting of my own sense of guilt about Art's death, despite our reconciliation only a few hours ago. "Here we go again, dog," but Brody is chewing so loudly he doesn't hear me.

Mr. Crandall writes that the company has abandoned the idea of suicide, that the disruption of the prescription of atenolol could possibly have been the cause of death, but after interviews with the physician and the coroner and the insurance agent who has interviewed the widow, they could find no evidence of willful intention to die on Mr. Finlay's part. The beneficiaries will receive their portions of the proceeds of the policy within two weeks. He thanks me for my assistance in putting this matter to rest.

I reread the letter, reach for the phone, and then put it down. The beneficiaries will get their own letters. It's no longer up to me to tell them that I am innocent in the eyes of California Mutual of causing my husband's death by suicide. I just need to believe it myself. I hear a voice whispering, "I'm sorry," and I do, at least for right now.

"Hellooo." Lynne's greeting sounds over Brody's crunching, and I open the door to find a glowing, joyful even, face grinning at me.

"What? I haven't seen you look this full of it since a mountain trip eons ago. Come in and tell me!"

"I know it's a bit early for champagne, but we're celebrating!"

I'm sure she's not celebrating my own tentative steps onto a new path, so it has to be... "You just won the lottery?" Damn. Her envelope was even better than the one Bob has brought to me.

"No! I'm getting married." Lynne takes the wine from its paper sack and plunks it on the counter. "Mumm's. Only the best for this momentous announcement. Where's a towel?" She grabs the one hanging over the faucet and unwinds the metal wire holding the cork. "I'm never sure how to do this. We may have to lick it off the Formica, but maybe you have a couple of glasses in case I don't mess up?"

I do, and I find a clean towel to wipe them off. I can't remember when I last took these crystal flutes out of the cupboard. "Married? I mean, congratulations, or is it best wishes to the bride? And who is the lucky...omigod, Wednesday/Saturday man?" At her nod, I understand that my dear friend is also coming to grips with a few of the realities life is handing her. I set the glasses down and wrap my arms around her, the bottle nestled between our breasts. "He's a patient man, friend. He's also a lucky man."

Then Lynne gets the cork out without too much overflow and pours the wine into our glasses. "Let's sit," she says. "I'll tell you all about it."

If I need a distraction from my obsession about a phone call from Brian, I get it. Lynne didn't experience any midnight absolutions to propel her into her decision. She tells me that she has a man who says he'll wait forever, but his preference is a closet next to hers, the shared daily paper over the daily morning coffee, and a funny, adventuresome woman to keep him anticipating what's next in his later years. "I know how all this ends," he told her. "I just want to know that each day will be a good as we can make it. Even if it means watching Golden Girls instead of football sometimes, even if it means cooking dinner once in a while, even if it means listening to you snore every night instead of twice a week."

Lynne sighs. "I don't snore,' I told him. 'Of course, you don't,' Wednesday/Saturday man assured me. 'Only a little,' I admitted. And somewhere in there," Lynne says, "the deal was sealed. I am tired of being alone, and he's a very nice man to spend the next ten years with."

"Ten years? Then?"

"We'll be lucky to live ten more years with a modicum of our selves still operating. After that, it's up for grabs. Everything's up for grabs."

"Then I'd better get busy." I empty my glass and hold it out for more. "I suppose it's too late for a facelift. Who'd believe an almost seventy-year-old lady with no wrinkles and blond hair. One or the other."

"Not too late for a lover," Lynne says. "Not kidding, friend...and by the way, how's Seth, that nice man from the restaurant?"

I talk too much about the coming Monday date with Seth, my menu, my fascination with his green eyes, and my new makeover cosmetics. I've had enough champagne to spend a moment or two reflecting on what I might do if things go further.

Suddenly, I can't talk about him anymore. Brian has taken over.

Lynne's enthusiasm melts in the middle of her sermon about safe sex. "Something I said? You suddenly went dead."

"Brian..." Then I plunge in. "My son, the perfect son, doesn't have the balls to tell his wife about a lost daughter with black hair, about Latisha's mother, of his and Art's involvement in a strange mess Brian created when he was still a kid.

Lynne doesn't flinch at these new details. She responds only to what she hears underneath my words. "We all were in messes when we were twenty. You were married for decades for the wrong reason, and I denied that the man I married was psychotic until someone else finally noticed and took him away. I believed that I had driven him crazy. But we came out of our messes pretty much okay, didn't we? Grew up, sort of; got a grip and have things to look forward to, now that our lives have gotten simpler."

I want to talk about Brian, not me. "But it's really hard when it's one's child who's in bad trouble. When he was little, I used to get in the middle, tell off the terrible teacher, point a finger at a bully and say, 'Stop it or I'll get you,' or whisper, 'Your father didn't mean it. He loves you,' to a child crying into his pillow. But now..."

"When they're small, it's a mother's business to protect her whelps. Edith, your son is a fully grown man. Whose business is it to take care of things? Not yours. Your job is to teach grandkids to make mac and cheese and to reassure them that their parents love them too much to abandon them. You're getting very good at grandmothering. Your other job no longer exists. You've been let go. You got your blue slip."

I am now drunk enough to move in next to my best friend and kiss her cheek. "Pink slip. Thank you, and...I'm very, very glad for you and the next ten years."

"Thank you. Will you be my matron of honor? In three weeks at my place. Dinner at your friend Seth's new restaurant."

35

Of course, Brody says in his silent way, you have a headache. And no walk for me last night. Thank Dog we have a backyard or you'd be stepping in it. And speaking of that, why were you sick in the toilet this morning? I only do that when I eat roadkill.

I should remember that champagne does a number on my body. But who can say no when a friend is so happy and wants to share her news? I wash down a couple of aspirins and try to focus on the Sunday paper, but I can't. Lynne has swerved in a way I hadn't seen coming, into marriage, commitment, a shared life. "For the next ten years..." she said. Then there's my next ten years. I haven't seen them coming either. She suggests that they will be filled with grandkids and whatever else walks into them. And whoever.

After my night time visit with Art, the relief I felt when I woke up, I'm pretty sure my husband is gone for good, except for the parts of him I find in our photograph albums and in the face of our son. But how do I move on, swerve into the next ten years? Not happening at this moment, I realize, as the phone rings, and I nearly knock the instrument off the table grabbing for it, hoping it is Brian calling.

It isn't. It is Seth confirming our Monday morning date and directions to my house. His voice is warm, a smile of a voice, and the disappointment I felt when I heard it melts. As soon as I hang up, I begin looking through my cookbooks for brunch recipes. I'm intimidated, of course, by Seth's expertise with down-home food. And I'm not going to do the strata—I am taking a little swerve here—so I search for more exotic dishes. An hour later, I've bookmarked: chakchouka, a Middle Eastern ragout; bao, a Chinese steamed bun; bubble and squeak, a cabbage/potato hash from England; and an omelet torte so complicated the recipe is described as the signature dish of a striving new restaurant. I like bubble and squeak because its name will make us laugh, but I don't have an iron skillet nor do I have any leftover roast beef. The ragout feels like dinner; the steamed buns scare me.

I'm left making a shopping list for the torte, which I see includes puff pastry. Shit. Too late. I've decided and that's it. Despite my past struggles with puff pastry, I'm going to make this torte even though I'll probably end up swearing. My mouth waters just reading the recipe. Only one small hitch—I tore the recipe out of the Oregonian. No mention of

its source. Maybe Seth? His chef? But he doesn't serve
breakfast. And puff pastry is not down-home, unless one is
French. I grab my bags and go to Fred Meyer.

It feels good to worry about something I can do something about.

A couple of hours later, I am home, and I have to make two
trips to my car to bring in the groceries. After I've unloaded
the bags on the table and can sit down for a breather, I consider pouring myself a glass of wine, early, hair of the dog,
when the flashing red light on the phone interrupts that
thought. It's heart-stopping, the fear that descends on me at
that moment. I have to close my eyes against it. I exhale,
know that I have managed for a few hours to be wholly myself. I planned a meal, and perhaps even more, was contented being led by the idea of a green-eyed man as I walked the
aisles of a grocery store. But here I am, back where I was
when I started this day. Lynne advised me that I am not a
mother any more. My child is an adult, she said. His problems are not my problems. Despite my disowning them, they
are squirming, inside me, making my stomach ache, causing
my body to slump as I lean against the counter for support.
I reach for the receiver.

A tinny voice informs me I have a dentist appointment
on Tuesday. Let the office know if I want to cancel—a robo
call from Dr. Seltzer.

I hang up. I don't know what to do next, but the bags of
groceries demand that I deal with them before the frozen
pastry goes bad. I pack the cheese, eggs, potatoes, onion into

the fridge and the box of puff pastry in the freezer. I fold and lay the sacks in the drawer. The counter is clear; the dog is asleep after a preliminary greeting. I'm tempted to collapse to the floor and howl like a banshee.

Something other than despair is roiling in my stomach, not hopelessness, not guilt. Anger again. Anger at a son who is screwing up not only his own life, but that of his children, his wife, mine. The only person who is not deserting him is his dead father, who, in a case of arrested fatherhood, came to his rescue, not once but again and again and maybe even now if he is visiting his son's dreams, too.

Stop it, I tell myself. You are finished with Art. Art the husband, yes, maybe, but Art the father—perhaps I'll never know what bloomed between them, and why in those last days he stood by his son's side and recouped his role as father. This is the mystery that is making me want to send a howl of warning of the death of my family to the moon.

I pour a glass of dry white wine. Perched on the tall stool at the counter, I take a cautious sip. Another. I look out the window. It's a gray day, not a day to sit back in one's blue lounger and dream. And, no banshee howl today. This is a come-to-Jesus day. I feel my lips moving. Silent words, fierce, satisfying as they burst out of my body, seek a target. I hope Art is nearby, listening.

No, I'm not finished with you, Art. I need to know why I, the mother, was not included in the secret that bound you and your son? Were you afraid I couldn't deal with it, that I would...what? Collapse in shock, go insane with the truth, hurt someone, become even more of a bitch from hell? Did you believe I wasn't strong enough to face the truth?

Well, the truth is right here, right now, and I am facing it, Art. The truth is that our son is a coward. You tried to help him, but all you did was support his cowardice, handing out money, offering your ear, and risking the small amount of trust that I might still have had for you. You failed. Art. And our son is fucked up.

I pour myself another glass of wine and thank HBO once again for that word.

"Seems like it, fucked up," Lynne agrees a few minutes later, "and the best part is that you called me instead of Brian to let off steam."

"It's hard, Lynne, flipping the mother switch off." I've had a third glass of wine and I've put the bottle away. In the morning I will be taking a first step into the next ten years with a torte, and I'll need all my senses to do this.

"Friend, I suspect as you wait for Brian to grow up, face his wife, become the man you believed he was, I suspect that you will be in for a surprise. Not only about him, but about yourself. This waiting for him to call you, to tell the truth, is the hard part. It will teach you that you are much more than a wife, a mother. You are a..."

"Stop. I gave a sermon like yours to my son when he was twelve and didn't get the part of Pinocchio in the school play. 'It will make you strong,' I said. 'Able to persevere in the face of disappointment.' Whoa. Look where it got him. All I need from you right now is to tell me what an asshole my son is." The wine is talking but the sentiment seems real.

"Sorry, I don't tell drunken ladies anything they want to hear. Except, go to bed. You have lots of puff pastry to conquer tomorrow, and a lovely man to let you know that deep down, you are okay no matter what you've thought and said tonight."

"I am okay. And I've decided at this very moment that I'm through waiting for my son to man up. I will introduce Latisha to her mother and father tomorrow afternoon, they in absentia, of course, at the meeting with Ginnie.

"Are you sure?"

"I'm too old to wait any longer. I've got a life, too, you know." I am a little drunk, but I've never felt more sure about a decision. "I'm doing this for me, not Brian. I advised him to take charge, but it is I who needs to take charge. Of my own life, not my son's."

"I'm so glad to hear you say that. About having a life, that is." I hear her murmur "Migod " to her Wednesday/Saturday guy as she hangs up.

I stumble over Brody who rolls his eyes at me and says, Careful. I'm about to explode unless you open the door.

I do and then we both decide we need to get some sleep.

36

I'm beginning to believe that swearing is an important in-
gredient of good cooking. I do a lot of it when I discover
that the puff pastry has to be defrosted before I can unroll
it, but it gives me time to chop the potatoes and onions,
cook them, whip up the eggs and cook them, twice, and then
get to the puff pastry, which turns out okay, puff-pastry-
wise. One sheet tears in half, but who cares when it's all
covered up by the time you get it out of the oven? I like the
rhythm of chopping peaches, bananas, oranges and pineap-
ple into a compote, and I thank the free trade agreement for
allowing these fruits to make it to my local market out of
season.

I've set the table with my old china, the kind fifty years
ago we almost-married young women chose for our trousseau

and received as wedding presents, one plate at a time. I love my pattern. I rarely use it, except at Thanksgiving. Birds in Trees. It was a hopeful theme for a marriage from which the actual birds disappeared, and most of the trees. Stop it. Cloth napkins. I smell something burning.

At the knock at the door, Brody stands up to defend me.

I can't see his face because it is blocked by a riot of yellow, purple, and orange tulips. I rise up on my toes in order to meet his eyes and say hello. He peeks over his offering. "Thanks for having me."

I've never received a bouquet before. African violets back when I set them on my windowsill and someone noticed, but not like this. I don't have a vase, so I take out one of my grandmother's dusty pitchers that didn't make it to Goodwill and wipe it off.

"You might want to cut off a few inches on the bottom," Seth says. "Lets them get to the water easier." Is there no end of ways this man will surprise me? I get the kitchen shears, and he clips off the stems, arranges the flowers and sets them in the middle of my lovely china setting. "Perfect,' he says, and it is. Except that something still seems to be burning in the kitchen.

"Oh, oh," I say as I open the oven door. Looks okay except for a smoking puddle of black crust on the oven floor. Leftover Thanksgiving cherry pie, maybe. "We're okay."

And indeed we are. We start with a fruity South American drink, thanks to the recipes that came with the blender, and we end up laughing and...well, I am limp, all parts of me, enthralled by his eyes that send lovely signals as we knife into the torte I'll be eating for the next week. And that will be just fine.

"I like your house, Edith. It speaks of you."

I'd like to say, "You should have seen it a few weeks ago when it screamed of me, antimacassars and all." But I just say, "I like it, too."

We move to the sofa for coffee and quiet calm fills me. I just want to lean back, sip my coffee and imagine. Seth disrupts my mood. "Latisha came by the restaurant last night, and she's excited about meeting her birth mother soon."

I don't like not understanding whatever he's talking about, so I tell him that I'm meeting with Ginnie and Latisha this afternoon. "Really? I thought I'd be able to help her move in that direction." I don't go on. I don't like the way Seth is sitting up a little straighter, holds his cup to his lips, doesn't speak.

"What?"

His beautiful eyes close. He knows something I don't.

"What?

"This has nothing to do with us, Edith."

Well, it kind of does, I want to say. He knows something about Latisha. About her birth mother. About plans to meet her. About Brian, too, maybe. It's obvious that Ginnie and her brother have been sharing information behind my back, maybe since the beginning. About Patsy? About Art? About Brian? About things I don't know?

"You're not telling me everything, are you?" I can't bear to look at him. I get up and move to the window. I want to raise my voice, but I swallow my words, try to sound sane.

"Any person I might want to get close to needs to know that I, for the next ten years at least, am going to demand No Secrets. Secrets are what screw up people. My family has been victimized by secrets." I give up on the swallowing. "How many secrets do you and keep, about my son, my husband, my granddaughter, me? What damage shall I expect next? "

He stands. "I'm not sure I understand...Latisha seemed so thrilled..." He reaches out to me. I push his hand off my arm.

"Thank you for the flowers, but I'm finished with secrets. Please leave." Seth is silent as he pulls on his coat, looks at me for moment and then walks out to the porch and away from me and my anger. Even Brody is confused by his abrupt departure. He paws at the door and sniffs. He likes this man who scratches his head under the dining table.

I'm not sniffing, but I also stand at the closed door for a minute, remind myself that I cannot trust a man who holds secrets. And maybe that's every man.

Something to consider, but first, I have to clean up the kitchen and get ready for a meeting with a teenage granddaughter and a social worker, and who knows what secrets that woman is holding, what side that woman's on? Why sides? I stop in the middle of scraping the rest of the torte into the disposal, the water running until I lower the handle. If there are sides, whose side am I on?

I've finished with Art and what he was up to. I have been advised that I cannot solve my son's problems by interfering or lecturing. I'm learning to love Kathleen, and I admire her decision to leave a lying husband, but she doesn't need my help—maybe later, with the kids. The only person I can stand next to, be on her team, is Latisha, who wants to meet her birth mother and maybe get to know her grandmother.

It's obvious when I sort it all out in those terms. This afternoon, for certain, it will be I who tells Latisha who her birth mother is, and who her father is, no matter how and when the social worker has intended to pass this information along. I owe it to a young woman who has a little me in her, in her naïve trust in people, in her dreams of going to college, becoming a teacher, maybe, or whatever. Her choice.

What a concept, I think. Choice.

I have no proof, I'll admit, only a story told me by a son who refuses to tell it again. I'll bring a picture of Latisha's father, compare chins if I have to, and eyes. Wide, trustworthy eyes. At least, until recently.

I drive up to the social services building fifteen minutes early and spot a coffee shop across the street. A latte will sit well on top of the morning's unfinished breakfast. After getting my coffee, I find a table next to the window, but I don't look at anything going on in the street. Instead, I turn inward, try to see at what will come next.

I am the star of the scenes that float behind my eyelids: me, outing my son to his daughter; facing him, his deceitful mother, when he discovers what I've done; me, realizing that the bonds we have built over the past forty years will be destroyed.

I'll lose a son and maybe gain a daughter. Possibly two daughters, if Kathleen, when she hears about this meeting, understands that I'm doing this for her, too. And, if it's true, I'm doing it for me, too, for the me I want to be for the next ten years, a woman who can make choices, who will face the scary "what if's" of her days. With ten years ahead of me, that's not an overload of "what ifs,"—just a short life of being true to one's self and seeing where it goes.

I dab at my tears with the crushed paper napkin I find on the table, not mine, but I don't worry about its origin. I have another vision. Me, eighteen, pregnant, finishing up my senior year in high school: Senior English, Hamlet. The teacher has just read a quotation that seems directed entirely at me, and I hide behind my textbook.

"To thine own self be true, and it must follow, as the night the day, thou canst not then be false to any man."

It's taken almost fifty years for these tears to rise to the surface, for the message to make sense. No more mask of wifeliness, complacency, helplessness, misplaced loyalty. No more being false to anyone, especially to myself.

I close my eyes again. When I open them I repeat, I'm going to be true to me. Now. The only people I care about are two almost-daughters who need me to walk out of this coffee shop and ride the elevator up the six floors to Ginnie's office. I push back my chair. Then I glance out the window.

Across the street, I see Brian and a tall, dark woman enter the building I'm headed for.

The caffeine bravura breaks down and I am left stranded, weak-limbed, confused at the curb. A coincidence, I tell myself. True to one's self, I repeat with each step, as I cross at the corner. I swallow the lump in my throat, push through the lobby doors. Brian and the woman have disappeared. I press the button for the sixth floor and the doors open. I ride up not knowing what I'll find or what I'll say in the social worker's office.

The reception room is empty except for a paper-sorting woman at the desk. She'll let Ginnie know I'm here, she says. "She's expecting you." And as I wait, I hear Brian's voice behind the office door.

37

Ginnie Washington, in a green suit this time, opens the door, waves me into the room. Brian, Latisha, and that woman are seated around the conference table. Latisha's brown eyes widen when she sees me, her lips begin to curve. "Edith," she says. "Come sit by me." I take the chair at her side.

I'm aware that Ginnie is speaking, sounding like the social worker she is. "Let me introduce you two, Patsy Walker, Mrs. Finlay, Brian's mother." I automatically reach for a dark hand that is coming at me from across the table. The touch is soft, fleeting. Her damp palm tells me she is as nervous as I am. Her black hair is flecked with gray, her eyes are somber.

"I'm glad to meet you," I say. I can't tell if I'm smiling. I turn to Ginnie. "What is happening?"

"Mom..." Brian begins, but Ginnie interrupts him.

"I received a call yesterday from your son who told me that he understood that Latisha would be coming here today, perhaps to learn about her parentage, that you would be here also. He informed me that this was his, not your, responsibility, and said he would be here also, with Latisha's birth mother. He asked me to let his daughter know that they were eager to meet her." The social worker turns to Latisha. "And when I called Latisha to tell her this news, she said she'd been waiting for this for a long time."

Ginnie pauses. "So here it is: The woman sitting across the table from you, Latisha, is your mother, Patsy Walker." The girl rises out of her chair with a small cry. Ginnie continues, "And this man," and she holds her hand out to my son, "is Brian Finlay, your father. They have come today to meet their daughter."

The three of them push back chairs, hurry towards each other, gather at the end of the table, and hesitate. Then Latisha says, her voice childlike chirp, "I want to hug you both. May I?"

Brian, Patsy, and Latisha lean into each other, and I hear someone sob. Me.

When the group breaks up, Ginnie asks them to sit down once more. "Someone else is also part of this reunion today, perhaps even the cause of it. Latisha," her hand extends in my direction, "this is your grandmother whom you know as Edith."

"Grandma Edith," I correct her. The words come as easy as a sigh. "Welcome to our family. I'm so glad you have found your parents." I reach out and take her into my arms. I would like to add that I'm also glad I have found my son. And that my son has found himself. I'll tell her that story another day.

Across from me, Patsy's face is wet with tears.

"It's wonderful, isn't it, to find a child?" I ask her. Patsy is still absorbing Latisha with her eyes.

"You don't know how wonderful," she says. But I can guess.

Latisha is still clutching my hand. "I don't really under-stand all this." She glances around the table. "Ginnie, can you explain? How...?"

"Brian is the one who knows this story best."

And for the next hour my son, strong in a way I had on-ly hoped for, looks from his daughter to her mother, and tells how he met Patsy, how he abandoned her when she told him she was pregnant, and how he found her later when she asked for help. "That's when I realized I had a daughter, you, Latisha." He went on to explain that years later he asked his father, Art Finlay, for help to find her. "I wanted to know what kind of girl you were, and when my father found you, he told me you were the best kind of girl—smart, pretty, level-headed. He insisted we help you with college money."

Latisha's smile wavers. "And how did you learn about me, Edith?"

I clear my throat, flinch a little as I answer. "I was jealous. I thought Art had been leaving the house in the evening to see another woman. Following a few clues, I discovered that he was—you." An embarrassing snort interrupts my words. "I wasn't that great a detective. I thought you were either his lover or his daughter." I don't go into my guilt over Art's death, my fear that I'd driven him to suicide. This girl is strong, but these are some more things she doesn't need to know right now. And it's Brian's job to talk about the need to keep it all a secret.

Patsy stirs, her voice gentle but determined. "Brian and I met at work, Latisha. We went out a few times, but then I got pregnant. With you. He was getting married. Our relationship didn't mean anything to either of us. He supported me for a few months before I had you and you were adopted. Years later, I was drinking, was deep into drugs, really sick, and I needed money to feed my habits. I went to Brian and he paid for rehab that didn't work. I was twice as bad off last fall when I threatened to tell his wife about you, not that I knew where you were, if he didn't give me money." Patsy looks down at her clenched hands on the tabletop and stops talking for a moment. Her chin rises with a deep breath. "He sent his father to find me. They planned to buy me off once and for all."

"That plan didn't really work out," Brian interrupts. "What did work is that your grandpa found you, with Ginnie's help. And a while later, Patsy on her own found the courage to get clean. She wanted to meet you, Latisha. So she asked for help again, and went into treatment where she has gone through hell and has come out the other side." His palms rise above the table, include us all. "And here we are."

Patsy, smiling finally, adds, "I'll be leaving the half-way house in a couple of weeks and I'll be ready to go to work and school, live a different life, and maybe, if you want," and she looks at Latisha, "practice being a mother."

"That sounds okay." Doubt colors Latisha's words. I can guess what's going through her mind. Another mother. The girl has had too many mothers. It will take a while for her to trust a new one. And she doesn't have the full story, maybe never will. We've left a lot of details: Patsy's sordid life until lately; Brian and the mess his own life has become in the past three months; guilt, mine, his, not part of Latisha's story, the one we are telling her now.

Ginnie closes her files. "Yes, it is okay. May I suggest a family dinner, the four of you, to get acquainted and to figure out what is next? No hurry to make decisions, though. You've waited years for this moment. Enjoy it."

Latisha grins, maybe relieved at the "No Hurry" Ginnie has introduced. "I was so nervous I haven't eaten anything all day," she admits. Her several parents chuckle.

Brian leans back in his chair, relieved, too, I'm sure, for perhaps the same reason. "Why not? Dinner's on me."

"And there's new restaurant just a few blocks away. You've been there, haven't you, Edith?" The social worker's green eyes turn to me.

And once again I am reminded that somehow Ginnie knew what I was going to tell Latisha at this meeting, and why Brian has come to face his daughter. As I suspected, Seth and his sister have been talking all along, maybe since before Art's death, as he searched for an eighteen-year-old girl. When Art sent me out into the streets, following matchbooks and credit card receipts, looking for clues, they knew the answers to questions I didn't know I was asking. Art must have told Ginnie about the bracelet, about blackmail. When I hinted this morning that I intended to help Latisha find her parents, Seth had warned Ginnie. This meeting wasn't according to their plan, one in which I wasn't included. Perhaps they thought I'd be angry, muddy the waters, that I would operate on my own, not according to some sort of social worker protocol. They decided to end the confusion before it got out of hand. They called Brian.

Brian is here not because of an inner sense of right. He's up against a wall, forced to come clean. Just as he would have been had I done what I intended as I drank that cup of coffee across the street. Only not so tidily, loose ends tied up, file closed.

I am sick to my stomach. Secrets. I am about to stand up, leave, but as I reach for my purse once again hanging on the back of my chair, I am struck with the understanding that what I had hoped to accomplish, the revelation of the truth, has happened. Without me. I will not allow my own feelings of betrayal by Seth and Ginnie to spoil this moment. Nor will my disappointment in my son.

"Yes, I have been to Magnolia. It's great." I ease the straps of the purse over my shoulder, join the others who are also rising from our secret-free circle.

The restaurant has a table for us, and we order right away. I glance around and do not see Seth. We seem a little uncomfortable, we parents, that is. Latisha, smiling for real now, asks Patsy about her life, where she lives, who does her hair. She asks Brian about his family, and he describes Winston and Meg, her half siblings and promises she'll meet them. Soon. And we sneak glances at each other, and I try to make sense of the form this new family will take. Christmas? Strata?

And then I can't do it anymore, this cheerfulness. We have not mentioned a wife standing with her back to us on the sidelines. Certainly, Brian has not offered even a hint of her existence. Perhaps she actually is missing. I can't stand the thought, and I'm glad when it's time to slip on our coats. Brian and Patsy set dates, different times, I notice, for visiting Latisha at her apartment. Patsy and Latisha decide to ride the bus to Cuppa's and talk more, and Brian walks me to my car, parked close to his.

"I like Patsy," I manage to admit as Brian opens my car door for me. "She's a survivor. Gutsy. Latisha has her eyes." I dare to pat his cheek as I would have years ago. "It's good that you've helped her, that she is recovering."

Brian cracks a grin for the first time in days, I'm sure, and the dark feelings that have infiltrated my soul begin to melt. "You sound like my mother again," he says.

And he sounds like my son. And I can't resist. "There's more to be done, son." I'll find out how this meeting came about at another time. Brian is not yet finished with an important part of his story.

"You really do sound like my mother again." Brian leans through my open window and brushes my cheek with his lips. "I know what you are saying. I had to make things right before I told Kathleen. I had to take care of Latisha and Patsy first. They were my problem, not hers." He looks at me with his serious, unflinching eyes. "It's going to be okay, Mom." He gives my car a goodbye knock on the roof and walks away.

When I get to my house, Brody is panting. Either he has to go out or he is telling me a voice mail has gotten him excited. I decide on the first possibility, and we go for a walk, both of us taking in the quiet, starry evening and the smell of new grass.

I have my pajamas on when I notice the red light flashing on the voice mail button. I

hesitate, then press the button. Seth's voice: "Once again, our meal ends prematurely. And once again, it seems to be something I've said that sends one or the other of us out the door. How about this: We meet and we don't eat. We talk. Or I don't talk. Probably an even better idea. Let me know when next you walk Brody, and I'll meet you at the dog park. I know Brody will like that, and so will I. My home number: 503-163-1328."

I erase the message and his voice. If he and his sister have been sharing my family's secrets, we have no future. No secrets. Even though their indiscretion has accomplished what I had hoped for, a son who is shedding his own secrets.

38

The next morning, her hair, hanging in wormy tangles, drips across her cheeks and onto her jacket collar. Her eyes, red and puffy, squint at me through the screen door. Kathleen has never seemed so miserable as at this moment, and she sounds even worse. 'Mom, I just can't stand it. I need your help."

I let her in, lead her by her moist arm to the sofa, push her a little to make her sit down. "Let me get a towel." The rain rattles against the open bathroom window, has leaked onto the sill during the night. I close the sash, pull two towels out of the cupboard and rush back to my sodden daughter-in-law, "What? What has happened?"

Kathleen lets me strip her of her jacket and wrap a towel around her head. I dab at her cheeks and wet knees, and a thin wail escapes her. "I love him, Mom. And I miss our life. The house is lifeless without him, and I am empty. The children, with such sad eyes, are empty, waiting for him to come back." She's crying so hard her words burble out in spurts. The towel on her head tilts and drops to her shoulders and she uses a corner of it to wipe her nose. "I don't know what to do."

"Have you talked to him...lately?" What is Brian waiting for? He was so certain yesterday, ready to come clean to everyone, it seemed like. But not to his wife? Why not?

"He called this morning, asked how the kids are, said he wanted to pick them up after school, take them to dinner because he hadn't seen much of them lately. That's all he said, except to ask where I was in the divorce proceedings. He needed to get his lawyer involved so he wanted my lawyer's name. I gave it to him. He hung up. It all became so suddenly real." Kathleen hiccups once or twice and wipes her eyes on the towel.

I don't know what to say. I can't stand watching her suffer, believing that any of this misery was her fault. It was, and still is, Brian's fault for not trusting that his wife could handle the truth. I could tell her the story right now, over the cup of coffee I'm handing her, let her in on the not-so-secret secret, tell her the reason her marriage is about to fall apart. Not knowing is always the worst part. It breeds such terrible guilt. I still feel it, the guilt nestling down behind my breastbone. Even though I know the truth.

"Sometimes what seems real turns out to be a fairy tale, a story we make up to explain the mysteries. What if the orange smell, the late nights, the money, what if all those mysteries are part of a myth you've created? What if the explanation is right around the corner, waiting for you to walk by?" Or, right next to you on this sofa, cup in hand? I am one sentence or two from ratting on my son. I hesitate when I feel Brody's tongue on my leg. He needs to go out. I put my cup down and stand up walk to the back door. "Saved by a dog's lick," I say, out loud, I guess, because Kathleen calls, "What?"

By the time I get to back to the living room, I know I cannot tell Brian's story. He has to, not his mother.

Kathleen has folded the towels and is running her hand through her damp hair "I feel better. You're right. I've concocted a story that is built on nothing but fragments of distrust." I see a flicker of the strong woman who stirs within the wet, blotchy body now pulling on a jacket. "Before I give up completely on my marriage, I need to know the facts, decide if they are worth the kind of sadness that is making me crazy this morning. I'll see him tonight. He owes me an explanation." At the door she adds, "I won't let him leave without giving me one."

Should I call Brian? No. Kathleen, wet or dry, can do it much better than I. I go to the door, let Brody in, wipe his paws.

39

"I've decided to love my wrinkles," I tell Lynne when she answers the phone.

"That's good," she says. "You've earned them. What else is new?"

"We should go shopping for a bride's matron's dress." I'm experimenting with the idea that pleasant thoughts will be a salve for the painful ones lying just under the surface. "Maybe plan a little party before you take the leap; invite Sherry and Eleanor and your sister and others to send off your marriage vessel with a christening of wine and giggles?" I'm trying too hard and she knows it.

"So what's really on your mind, Edith?

I begin to tell her of Kathleen's visit, her tears, my decision to not reveal the secret I know, and of the meeting on

Monday, when I hear a click on the line. "Someone is trying to get through. I'll call you back right away." I never do that to friends, but I'm wired so tight I'm close to suffocating. I push the button. "Yes?"

"You sound funny, Grandma. What are you doing?"

It's Meg. "I'm practicing breathing. How about you?"

"We want to bring pizza by tonight and watch Nickelodeon. Daddy says he'll bring us by. Is that okay?"

"I'd like that. Come as soon as you can."

"Daddy says it'll be in an hour or so, and that we should bring our homework so you can help us before the TV."

"I'll do my best. Is your father there?"

"No, he talked on the phone to Mom and then talked to us. She says it's okay with her."

The hesitation in these last words signals an uncertainty about who's in charge. Sounds as if Kathleen is, at this moment. Hope she got her hair dried for this evening's event, and maybe a little makeup. Helps to feel beautiful when facing the unknown. At least that's what Pretty Woman taught me. That thought reminds me to call Lynne back.

"Geez, I never thought you'd do that," she says. "Hang up when we were about to discuss baggy eyes and snaky hand veins."

"Actually, we were discussing a couple of marriages, including yours and the one that's making me nuts."

"So are you still nuts after the call?"

"More so. Let's change the subject. Is it true that Preparation H will make bags under one's eyes disappear? Or is that a myth?" There it is again, that word.

"I had a friend who tried it. Her bags disappeared but her cheeks tightened up like Joan River's third facelift. She couldn't open her mouth. She learned later that she rubbed in a bit too much, maybe half a tube, in an effort to look forty again. Much classier to wear slightly tinted glasses with terrific frames."

"Okay, we covered that subject, and I'm assuming you'll call when you want to go shopping for a dress for me, but give me a day or so to get over whatever is happening in my son's life."

"Not your problem, friend. Remember."

"That's become my mantra." Not a very good one, though. Despite my attempt at being cheerful, I'm close to tears. "Why can't I just let go?"

"Pizza and a couple of happy TV watchers will help that. No matter what happens to that family, you have become a beloved grandma. Kids need grandmas. To go to when things get weird at home."

"What if the grandmas are weird?"

"All grandmas are weird. Veiny hands, blond hair that doesn't match anyone one else's in the family, wrinkly pokable cheeks, ancient word processors, and shelves of terrible records, yellowed-paged books, stupid games, and sometimes, jars of cookies, pizza without olives, soda pop, ears that listen without criticism, warm breaths as they say 'Good night, don't let the bed bugs bite' and she lands a kiss right on a grandchild's lips."

"Damn. I feel better." And I'm pretty sure I do. We hang up, and I wait for Winston and Meg to arrive. When they knock, they've come alone to the door, pizza-box smell preceding them, their father waving a hand from the car.

We play Crazy 8's, eat pizza and watch a silly Disney movie, walk the dog, look over three math sheets, and it is bedtime. They agree to go to sleep here at my house, until Daddy picks them up. I find two old T-shirts in my bureau. "Okay? These'll make it easier when your father comes; you can go home in them." And I discover two tooth brushes in a drawer, new, from Art's and my last dentist visits. "I'm afraid you'll have to share a bed," I say as they come T-shirted into my bedroom. "With me. At least until I've read you a story." I lie down in the middle, and the children climb in on each side of me.

"What story?" Meg asks.

I've found another book in the box in the hall closet. "This is one I read to your father a long time ago. It's kind of old, but you might like it. The Little Prince."

"We have that! Daddy has read it to us."

I reflect for a moment on the strands that tie us together, the books, the meals, the memories. "Good." And I begin.

"The End," I whisper a long time later then close the book and climb out at the foot of the bed so I don't disturb my two bewitched listeners. Meg dozes with a frown, and I lean over her to kiss her, and she sighs. Winston peeks at me from under half-closed lids when my lips touch his. "Good night," I say. "Don't let the bed bugs bite."

"Light," Winston whispers. I leave the door open, the hall light on.

When the phone rings an hour later, I expect it to be Brian, but it isn't. "I need to tell you something," Lynne says. She sounds all clogged up, like she's been crying, and I get ready to hear that Wednesday/Saturday man has backed out. "Get me a Kleenex, honey," she says to someone so I guess he's still around.

"What?" I ask. "You sound awful."

"I feel awful. I did something, I shouldn't have done. I thought I was being helpful, a friend. After I kept telling you to let Brian go, I got worried about you, how you might let whatever was going on with him mess up your own life, how you might even lose him if you did what you said you were going to do—narc on him, you know? Maybe even lose Kathleen and the kids." Lynne blew her nose, sniffed, said, "Oh God."

"Shit, Lynne. Just say it and get it over with."

"It felt like you all were tied up in one big knot, no way for anyone to get it untangled. Unless I reached in and gave a string a yank. Brian. Brian was the string. I called him. Told him what you were going to do." Her voice is a whisper now. "I'm so sorry if I fucked things up." She stops talking. In the background I hear a male voice. "Breathe, sweetie. It's going to be just fine."

I close my eyes, so relieved I can't talk either. Not Seth! Then I say "Yes!" so loudly Brody raises his eyebrows at me. "Yes. Breathe, friend. It's going to be just fine." And I tell her about the meeting, about the kids in my bedroom, and I begin to believe it too.

As we are about to hang up, the tangled knot almost un-done, Lynne murmurs, "I guess I did okay, then?" And I answer, "Indeed. Very okay," and both of us sigh "Love you" as we hang up.

A moment later the phone rings again. I hope to hear my son's voice. Seth's greets me. "You've had a big week. I hope it's all worked out for you."

I'm no longer annoyed that he knows something of what has been happening. He is interested. In my family. In me. I had hinted at my plan and he kept it to himself. He is trustworthy. "I don't know if it's worked out. In fact, Meg and Winston are here, in my bed now, and their parents are somewhere talking. At least I'm guessing that's what they're doing. My role is to heat the pizza and read The Little Prince, and I've done both grandmotherly tasks. Right now, I waiting for one of their parents to come pick up the children and maybe to let me know what's next."

"A difficult moment. I won't keep you, but I would like to go for a walk with you and Brody very soon. I find I miss you, Edith."

"Brody misses you, too."

Seth chuckles. "Not exactly what I meant, but it will do for now. Tell Brody I'll be by in the afternoon. I'll call him first."

40

I am cold and reach for the throw on the back of the sofa. My other arm is caught under a cushion this time, and I pull it out and rub away the cramp. I must have fallen asleep. I check my watch. It's after midnight. My heart contracts in a flurry of panic. The kids. I stumble to the bedroom, squint into the half-dark and see two bumps under the quilt, back to back as if they have agreed to ignore each other's wiggly bodies.

I head for the phone. In my midnight breathlessness, a thought skims across my forehead. Something's wrong. Maybe one of them hurt the other; maybe they are in the ER, unable or unwilling to phone. I blink and get rid of that scene. Stuff like that only happens in the Oregonian to really angry, sick people. Well, I think, as I pick up the receiver. They weren't that angry— maybe sick, though.

"Stop it," I say out loud. "If anyone's sick, it's me."

A voice crackles in my ear. "Mom? Are you there? I didn't hear the phone ring."

Brian. "Where are you? I've been worried." That is a little lie, of course. I've been asleep until five minutes ago. But still...

"We're here at home. And everything's okay, Mom, like I told you it would be. Everything. Are the kids asleep?"

"Everything?"

The phone rattles, and I hear Kathleen's voice. "Everything, Mom. Brian told me the whole story, about Patty and Art and Latisha, and how he kept it all a secret until he had taken care of it all, so I wouldn't be hurt. But the mystery itself hurt, like you said, not knowing is worse than knowing."

Mysteries. Myths to explain them. Truth-telling to destroy them. Maybe someday over a glass of wine I'll hear more about the telling of the truth that went on this evening. None of my business, though. But I have to ask, "So no other woman?" I know the answer, of course, but I want to find out if she understands that I also have kept back the truth from her.

"Only a new daughter. I'm not sure what I'll do when I meet her and her mother. Brian says you know them both, that you like them. Maybe we can all...God, I'm exhausted." She pauses, and I hear Brian whisper something. She answers, "Brian, no, I...okay...Mom, we wonder if the kids can stay until tomorrow. They can miss school..."

Kathleen is not angry with me for keeping the secret. I'm glad because I don't know what I'd do if I lost her. "Of course, you deserve a break from parenthood. For one night, at least." I rub my still aching arm, consider going back to sleep on the lumpy sofa. It will be worth it—my contribution to the resurrection of my family. "Come by around noon. Maybe I'll have time to make a strata to celebrate."

It's too late to call Seth and invite him too. I'll do it when Meg and Winston wake me up in the morning. I know Brody will be glad if his friend comes. I'm sure the rest of us will also be glad.

ACKNOWLEDGEMENTS

I so appreciate my first readers from writing group several years ago who reviewed the first pages of Never Too Late and got me started on the right track with encouragement and corrections about the accuracy of the medications and insurance. When the story seemed as finished as I could take it, I asked Janet Young and Peggy Bird, both great readers, to critique the story. Their comments inspired several re-writes and edits, thank God. Their continuing interest in the book kept me working on it, as did my patient husband who is a walking Thesaurus and is a handy person to yell at, like "What's the name of those green things I put on salmon?" when I suffer a word block. Thank you, Don, for being in the next room and always answering, "Capers!"

ABOUT THE AUTHOR

After graduating from Willamette University, Jo spent the
most of next thirty years teaching, counseling, mothering,
wifing, and of course, writing.

Her writing first appeared in small literary magazines and
professional publications. Since retirement, she has had time
to write four novels and two screenplays.

Her stories and essays, as well as the novels, reflect her
observations of women's lives and the people who inhabit
them: the children, husbands, parents, friends, and strangers
who happen by and change everything.

*Do you love the Penner Publishing book
you've just finished?*

Great books deserve great readers.

Please review this book on your favorite retailer,
bookish site, blog or on your own social media.

Penner Publishing is a boutique publisher
specializing in women driven fiction. We love our
romance heroines saucy or sweet. We also love a
great story even when there isn't a hot hero
involved. It's all about the woman's journey.

Be sure to visit us at:
www.pennerpublishing.com/readers-club
Facebook.com/pennerpub
Twitter.com/pennerpub